BODY ON THE TRACKS

Barbara Schlichting

Body On The Tracks

Formatting by Rik – Wild Seas Formatting

FIRST LADY PRESS

First Ladies Mystery Books
Dolley Madison: the BLOOD SPANGLED BANNER
Mary Lincoln: IF WORDS COULD KILL
Edith Roosevelt: the CLUE OF THE DANCING BELLS

Poetry
Whispers From the Wind

Picture books
Red Shoes — Barbie Marie (pseudonym)

Dear Reader, the Zephyrettes were used to promote train travel. They fulfilled the need of a nurse or in modern day terms, an airline steward. They had to conduct themselves in a dignified manner. The role was suspended during WWII. However, the first Zephyrettes appeared on the Denver Zephyr, then the Twin Cities Zephyr. After the war years, only the California Zephyr resumed its practice of employing the Zephyrettes.

During WWII, prisoners of war were held in the United States. Since the Midwest farm boys were at war, young laborers were few. It wasn't too uncommon to have a prisoner work on a nearby farm.

This book is dedicated to my grandpa, Carl Lindquist, who was an engineer on the Twin Cities Zephyr, and employed by the Milwaukee Road and Burlington Railway.

I also would like to thank two people who sat with me for hours when I was a beginning writer. Dwight Lewis worked tirelessly with me to shape up this book by reading, editing and offering suggestions. I baked pies and cookies for Dwight and his wife, Ginger. Linda Tappe left her kids for her husband, Tom to watch as we sat many times while I read parts of my manuscripts to her over coffee.

Grandpa

The six-foot, blue eyed Swede
stood next to his locomotive,
holding a small hand

The brown-eyed, blonde little girl
with a pony tail,
wrapped her arms around her grandpa's neck

He looked at his pocket watch,
then nodded to the conductor
and switchman

He handed the little girl to his son,
before kissing the top of
granddaughter's head

Goodbye.

TABLE OF CONTENTS

Chapter One

October, 1943

Day One

Brita woke as the depot clock chimed eleven times. She felt confused before remembering that she was in the Chicago's Union Station hotel.

Brita's stomach growled as she reached for her bakery roll, but she wasn't able to find it in the dark. She remembered Mr. Mindel, the passenger who had given it to her before he disembarked the Twin Cities Zephyr. Mr. Mindel had been a close family friend when she'd lived in France, and Brita wondered if her father hadn't assisted in his defection to the United States.

A rail yard light guided her steps to the window where she saw the shadows of passengers entering the lobby. The Twin Cities Zephyr had already departed for its return to St. Paul/Minneapolis. She'd worked as a Zephyrette on it, running up and down the cars helping passengers, especially the women with children. Goose pimples traveled up and down her arms as she looked out at the Burlington's Denver Zephyr. It shone like a comet in the night sky. She couldn't wait for morning when she would be part of the crew as it left for its final destination of Denver. Excitement flooded through her. She'd be able to meet and greet so many more immigrants, using her knowledge of languages as she helped them. The notion reminded her of her childhood growing up on military bases all over Europe.

As Brita's gaze followed the length of the silver Zephyr

toward the rear parlor car, she saw two men. One was tall and thick; his suit coat fit like an oversize glove. The other man was shorter, with a narrow frame and shoulders that sloped like a coat rack. He looked almost identical to Mr. Mindel, the man who had given her the roll. It appeared as if the taller man walked with a slouch and had a gun to the shorter man's back. She cupped her eyes against the light reflection and peered harder, noting Mr. Mindel's unmistakable limp. The gunman had a cigarette drooping from the corner of his mouth. Suddenly, he grabbed Mindel's tie. She watched as the taller man pulled the tie over Mr. Mindel's head before shoving it inside his own suit pocket. He then shoved Mr. Mindel down the Zephyr corridor and deeper into the yard.

"Run, Mr. Mindel!" Brita beat the window with her fist. "Help!" she screamed.

She slipped quickly into her skirt and top, dropping her knife and room key into her jacket pocket before pulling an army green stocking cap over her blonde curls. She knew the ground outside was wet and sloppy, so she slipped on rubber boots.

Brita kept within the Zephyr's shadow. She gazed up at her window and gauged where she'd seen the men.

Studying the ground, she found footprints. Brita followed them to the rear of the Zephyr. It wasn't long before she'd lost them because of the many sets of tracks. She got down on her haunches and studied the ground before moving slowly beyond the depot. Off to her left, she heard the distant sounds of cars honking and approaching train whistles. The bright yard light illuminated the footprints once again, with the help of the muddy ground.

The deep-set footprints led her toward a small remaining grove of trees and away from the nearby stockyard stench. Twigs snapped as she walked over toward some old oak trees. Angry voices drifted over the soft trickle of a nearby stream. A train *chunk-a-chunked* over a nearby track. Brita hid behind the branches to listen as the voices grew louder. She noted the language was German, which she understood, but the voices were too muffled to hear properly.

The larger man struck a match, a dot of the orange glowing in the shadows. Brita inched closer. Tripping over a tree root, she groaned as she tumbled to the ground. The snapping branches and rustling leaves cracked like fireworks on the Fourth of July in the quiet surroundings.

Brita shut her eyes tight as her heart beat like a drum. She crouched in the middle of a clump of trees and listened. A gunshot blast echoed in her ears, masking the sound of approaching soft footsteps.

*****

The killer circled the area where he'd heard the noise and spotted a crouching figure. Not having the noise of a convenient train running by to hide another shot, he struck his stalker on the head with the butt of his gun.

Grabbing the unconscious person's head, he pulled off the stocking cap, releasing a cascade of blonde curls. Stopping in surprise, he swore in German as he realized his snooper was the Zephyrette, Brita Torgerson. The daughter of his nemesis, the American, General Nels Torgerson.

Brita moaned, and he cracked her once again on the side of her head. Grinning, he slid off her underwear and stuffed them in his pocket. Leaving her face down, he took another good look at her sweet, exposed ass before walking away.

*****

Captain Ron Healy heard someone calling from Brita's room. His room was right next to hers, as requested by the general, since there'd been three escaped Nazis from an Iowa farm. The German POWs had been forced into service helping with the harvest since all able-bodied young men were enlisted in one of the armed forces. He'd been assigned to guard the Zephyrs. The POWs committed crimes as they escaped. They'd jump onboard passing trains and arrive at their destinations undetected before authorities became aware of the matter. General Torgerson had also asked him off the record to keep an eye on his daughter, but to "keep his fucking hands off her."

She was beautiful.

He cracked his knuckles before removing his OSS badge from inside his heavy coat pocket. His new assignment was to work undercover as a bartender, which actually sounded like a vacation. The last assignment was with the French Resistance, where he'd helped Dr. Fortier, who'd discovered the matrix for nuclear fusion, escape to the United States. General Torgerson had recommended him for the assignment to his superiors. However, Dr. Fortier had been missing from his work at the University of Chicago since August.

Ron sat on the bed and decided that Brita was probably in the bathtub and the water was too hot, perhaps the cause of the shouting. He let his thoughts go to his previous assignment. Once again, his beloved fiancée came to mind as his head swam with memories of her. After a few brief moments of solace, guilt washed over him like a welcome winter storm, assuring him that his conscience remembered correctly. Margot's death had been his fault. She'd told him that her cover was compromised, but he'd thought he could take just one more assignment and they'd be able to leave. It didn't happen. She'd been murdered by a German informant disguised as a French spy.

As he brushed his teeth to ready for bed, he heard someone calling and pounding on Brita's door. He glanced at his watch. Eleven-thirty.

*****

The squishy leaves felt moist under her belly. Brita squirmed. A sharp, brisk wind blew across her rear, and suddenly she realized that her skirt was up in the air. She tried to breathe deeply. There was a distinctive sour odor that was unrecognizable, but she attributed it to the wet ground. Brita gasped when she realized that her underwear was missing. Tears streamed down from her eyes and windblown hair stuck to her cheeks. Sweat trickled down her neck. Brita vowed silently that when she found out who had done this, she'd kill him with her own hands. Traces of fear trickled up and down her spine as she began to wonder if the assailant would return. She breathed a sigh of relief that her assailant hadn't gone that far.

A shrill train whistle gave her a clue as to the depot's direction. Brita stood, brushing her skirt down before pulling her jacket tight across her chest. She began to walk slowly toward the depot. The trees blocked the moon's glow, so it was extremely hard to see. Tripping over a fallen branch and sprawling face down once again, she sobbed from frustration.

While she chastised herself for being such a fool as to follow the two men, Brita began to recall what she'd seen and heard. There had been the flash of a match and a heated conversation in German. She hadn't heard the exact words.

Sweat streamed down her brow, and her hair felt like wet straw against her scalp. She itched. Plus she smelled like a sewer. Holding her breath, Brita tried to not inhale through her nose so that she wouldn't vomit.

Her nerves crackled as her ears perked to every sound. Automobile motors and honking cars in the distance drowned out the silence. The blowing wind made tree limbs crackle and snap while leaves swirled around her feet. Something skittered across her feet as she took another step. She cursed the uneven ground that felt slick underfoot. A nearby rustling startled her, almost causing her to fall over once again. Too much imagination, she told herself, and she took another baby step. Suddenly a twig snapped, much closer to her location. Brita sucked in her breath while hobbling back to the nearest tree.

Chapter Two

Uneasy, Ron walked to the main desk and placed a call to Brita's room. When the tenth ring began, he replaced the receiver and chased back to his room, where he removed a set of skeleton keys from his suitcase. After trying a couple, he was able to open Brita's door. The light was still on, and her suitcase lay open on the bed, but the room was empty. Her open purse was resting on the night table and invited further scrutiny. Digging through it, he found her room keys missing. He sat on the bed for a short while and tried to sort out the puzzle. He saw the bakery bag and picked it up. Inside was a crushed chocolate roll with the receipt showing two purchased rolls. A woman would've eaten them immediately. Also, she wouldn't go anyplace without her handbag Ron's gut instinct led him to believe that she was in some kind of trouble.

After he left her room, Ron walked briskly up and down the corridors and around the large waiting room looking for Brita. As the last woman left the restroom, he went inside and checked the stalls. He began to wonder if Gladys, another Zephyrette, might still be in the restaurant even though it was midnight.

At that moment, Ron knew he had to find her. She should have been in bed. He didn't have a clue where else to look and headed for the dining room. Gladys was seated alone but in a dark corner.

"Gladys? You haven't seen the other Zephyrette, have you? What is her name?" Ron asked.

"No. I pounded on her door, but she didn't answer. Her name is Brita," Gladys answered. "We were supposed to meet for a piece of pie before bed."

Ron went in search of the railroad bull and found him near the roundhouse. He was dropping pennies he'd found on the tracks, from his pocket into a can.

"Damn kids," he growled. He looked up as Ron approached. "The train could jump the tracks from them putting pennies on top of the rail."

Ron asked, "Have you seen a young blonde woman out walking tonight? Just curious." He watched as the railway bull pulled the stogie from his mouth.

"Yep, a while back." He took a short puff from the stogie and held it between his thick fingers. "I would've told her that Al Capone called this town home and to go back to her room, but she never stopped for advice."

"Anything else?" Ron waited, hoping that there'd be something more. The thought of Brita looking for someone didn't make any sense.

"Headed up in that direction," he said nodding toward the north. He wiped his brow, then stuck the stogie back into the corner of his mouth, narrowing his brow as he studied Ron. "Two tipsy sailors headed up in that direction, too. They were singing about some dame. That's it." Walking away, the man farted like a racehorse.

"Thanks," Ron said, choking. He turned toward the given direction and hoped to find Brita before the two other men did.

Instinct had told Ron that she was in trouble, and now this proved it. Two drunken sailors, home on leave and soon being shipped out, were probably after dames. Brita was beautiful, and they'd probably try to take more than she'd want to give. As Ron started putting a theory together, he searched up and down the trains and inside all of the boxcars. He hoped his theory was wrong, especially the part about the girl.

*****

Brita fell over a tree root and landed face down in the mud. She felt like a skinned rabbit. Brita wanted to melt into the ground when she heard nearby voices. Suddenly she realized that they were practically standing right beside her.

"Hey Ax! Over here," someone said. He looked toward his buddy and motioned for him to come over. "I think we saw her someplace along here, right? See? There's footprints. We're heading in the right direction."

Ax used his Zippo lighter to look down on the ground next to his buddy's foot, and smiled. "John, we were right. I'd bet my right nut that she's around here."

"Maybe she's peeing behind the trees."

Brita's heart pounded so hard that she could barely hear. She wondered who the devil they were, where they'd come from, if they'd kill her or help her… and if they spoke German. Brita was beginning to understand the true meaning of "sweat like a pig." Sucking in a deep breath, she heaved herself up to her feet, and immediately began to crumble.

"At first I thought you were full of shit, old man, just like our CO, but not anymore," John said.

Brita fell backwards into a tree. Breathing heavily, she squeezed her eyes closed and hoped and prayed that they wouldn't hurt her.

The flicker of the lighter suddenly played across Brita's thin frame.

"Holy shit!" John said. "What the hell happened to her!" He stumbled on a root as he reached over to Brita and helped her stand.

She sucked in her breath, standing rigid. Her body shook with fear. She didn't know if she should be relieved that she had been found or not.

"Shit," Ax exclaimed. "She's a mess! Bet she's thirsty. Wanna sip of hooch?" He leaned into Brita to hear her answer. "She's mute," he stammered. Raising the bottle of whiskey to his lips, he took a swallow.

"You're stupid. Let's get her inside the depot and call the authorities. Name's John, in case you're wondering." He set his bottle down. "I'm not going to hurt you. I'm only going to lend you my arm."

"Yeah, then we'll party," Ax said, hiccupping.

Brita's good sense told her that they were up to no good, but her heart told her that they were harmless. Drunk, but harmless.

"Don't worry, honey," John reassured her once more. He reached for her hand.

"I'm Ax." He pushed John's hand aside. He turned aside and vomited. "Shit," he said. "Excuse me, ma'am."

Their breath smelled like a Milwaukee brewery. Her heart still pounded from fear, but shades of relief began to ease the anxiety. She rubbed her head where it had been hit. "Ouch!"

*****

Slurring male voices echoed above the rustling of leaves. Ron's worst nightmare began to play out in his imagination as he picked up his pace.

"Miss Torgerson? Let her go! Why are you mauling her? Why is she such a mess?" Ron shouted. He rushed towards them. "What on earth have you done?" He glared at the two sailors. "You'd better tell all right now, or your CO will hear about it." He gave her a closer look and asked, "They haven't hurt you, have they?"

Brita tried to talk, but was tongue-tied.

"You better not have touched her," Ron growled.

The two sailors didn't move.

"Huh? What?" John stood ready to salute. "John Standish, permission to speak." He stumbled backward against a tree, startled by the angry and commanding figure before him.

"Permission granted. What were you doing to her? Maybe you can explain?" Ron stared at the other sailor.

"They were..." Brita tried to speak. "If..." Her heart pounded, and she couldn't stand the odor surrounding her.

"Axel Cunningham. Ax for short." He burped and wiped his mouth on his sleeve before returning to attention.

"What did you say?" Ron said, looking at Brita.

"At ease, you two. I'm not military, anyway." He turned to

Brita. "Could you give me a rundown, please?" Ron asked. "Remember me? We nodded to each other when I peered out in the hallway at our hotel. I'm next door to you." He looked at the two sailors, and the one named John was reaching for the bottle on the ground. He shone the flashlight on him, and said, "Leave it there and stay where you are."

"We didn't do it." He hiccupped. "Sorry."

"Neither did I." Ax crossed his arms.

"Don't worry," Ron whispered to Brita. "We'll get this sorted out."

"Mr. Mindel. Have you seen him? I think he's been shot. I've been…" She reached into her pocket. "My knife is gone!"

"Knife?" Ron asked, puzzled. "Someone has been shot?"

"Yes! We must find him."

"I'm Ron, the new bartender." He stared into her eyes and noticed she looked pale. "Tell me what happened."

Clutching her stomach, Brita covered her mouth. "Oh no…" She crouched behind the tree to vomit. "I feel stupid," she said, making a face and wiping her mouth.

"Don't worry about it." To John and Ax, Ron said, "Who are you two, besides a couple of two-bit sailors?"

"That's exactly what we are," John said, nodding.

"It's true," Ax agreed. "Bums."

"They just stumbled upon me," Brita said, yawning. "I know they didn't do this." She took a deep breath and said, "Of that, I'm positive."

"I guess I have no choice but to believe you. You two can leave." Ron stepped back to get a better look at her and knew that his first assumption was correct. She was beautiful and in danger, and it was going to be harder than hell to keep everyone's hands off the general's daughter… including his.

"We're staying nearby," Ax said.

Ron watched as both sailors stumbled away.

"Tell me how you ended up here," Ron said.

"From my room, I saw a man pushing another man, and it looked like he had a gun." The moon cast a glow across his face, and she liked what she saw.

"Well… go on." Ron noticed that she was looking at him, just as much as he was looking at her. It was as if they were trying to convince themselves to trust the other.

"You see… I was curious and figured that maybe I could help in some way. I tried to get the railroad bull interested, but he appeared quite busy. I was able to follow, but then I tripped, snapped a few sticks and landed in a heap in a clump of trees. Then I heard a gunshot." She gave him a serious look, then sighed. "They were standing right over there, somewhere." She pointed to her left. Shivering, she crossed her arms.

"Did you see anyone else?" When she shook her head, he said, "Over there?" Ron shone the flashlight in the direction she had pointed. "I don't see anything."

"I'm not really sure myself, to tell you the truth." She took a deep breath, and said, "Well… from over there…" She glanced back and then to where she stood now. "I was looking in that direction."

"Are you sure?"

"Almost."

They heard the footsteps of the two sailors.

"She'll be fine," Ron called out to John and Ax.

"Well, okay," Ax said. He hiccupped. The two sailors continued walking toward the depot.

Ron turned back to Brita, and said softly, "I bet you want to go to bed and sleep forever?"

"Yes, and bathe. The monster gave me a chop on the noggin," Brita murmured. "What time is it?" she asked. "I am angry, plus I'm all dirty and have terrible bad breath from vomiting. I'm hungry. I have a headache. I almost feel as if I might vomit again. Are you through with me?" Her teeth chattered. "What time is it?"

The yard whistle blew, signaling that the next shift would soon start. Another train whistled in the distance and the ground underneath their feet rumbled.

"It smells out here. Must be the stockyards," Ron said. He

shined his light on his watch, and said, "It's two in the morning." Ron shifted the flashlight, its glow like a blanket across the damp ground… but he didn't see anything or anybody. "I don't see any footprints."

"There have to be some around here," Brita said. As she scrutinized the area, she didn't see any either. "I know that I'm not making this all up. I saw the two men. One had a gun. There was an argument, then there was a gunshot." She glanced up ahead and studied the area for signs. "I believe the victim was Mr. Mindel. I've known him since I was a little girl in France."

"Really?"

"Yes. He was a friend of my father's."

"Very interesting. You'll have to fill me in later. I wonder where…" Ron shined his light up ahead. "What about over that way?" He turned around. "I think I see something." To him, it looked like a body, but he wasn't sure. He hesitated a moment and stared. It was, he concluded.

"Are you through with me?" Yawning, she sneezed into her sleeve. "I need to go to bed." Brita began to step back. "I'm going to head back."

"I'll take you," Ron said, turning his attention back to her.

"I see Ax and John up ahead stumbling around."

"I want to search the area once more. Do you mind if they escort you?"

"That's fine. I just want to go to bed," Brita said. She yawned again.

He led her to the two men. "Here. Please escort our damsel in distress back to the depot." As he shined the flashlight on them, as she curtsied. He said, "Keep her in your sight all the way."

"My knees fell wobbly," Brita said.

"Take good care of her."

"Yes, sir." They saluted sloppily in unison.

"Oh, golly. My knights in shining armor," Brita said.

As they walked away, Brita stopped a moment and turned to look at Ron, who still stood watching them.

"Good night," she called.

Ron made sure that they were well on their way to the depot before following the stream back to the body. The victim was a male, and blood covered the corpse. His jaw slacked downward to his neck, while his nose and forehead showed shattered bone fragments through the ripped skin. Blood seeped out of each ear, matting his hair. One of his arms lay by his side while the other held his chest. His suit coat was still buttoned and his knees were slightly bent.

Crouching down, Ron carefully unbuttoned the man's coat, which revealed a missing necktie and belt. As he examined the facial area where the most blood was, Ron found that the bullet entry was under the man's chin. Clearly it was a small handgun, or his head would've been completely blown off.

Ron reached inside the man's suit coat pocket. His train ticket and wallet revealed his name as Jacob Mindel. *Brita was right.* The ticket showed that he'd boarded in Minneapolis and was traveling to New York. His identification papers didn't reveal any other news.

Ron ran his hands down Mindel's pant legs and pulled off his shoes. As he felt inside the soles for hidden items, Ron also tried twisting the heels, but neither held a secret compartment. Since the wallet didn't reveal any new evidence, he slid it back into the pocket then put the man's shoes back on.

He shined the flashlight across the footprints. He could tell where he and Brita had walked, plus he found the footsteps of the unknown assailant. He studied the area.

"Mindel, I'll find your killer," he vowed. *Brita may be in more danger than I initially suspected.*

His flashlight gave him plenty of illumination to cross the rail tracks and skirt over to the looming depot's front doors in search of a railroad bull. Ron came upon the same man that he'd previously spoken to.

"Sir?" Ron said, coming up to him. The man stood tall. He was large and round like a silo. "There's been a murder I need to report. It's north of the tracks. The body is lying near the stream."

"What? Another one? Those gangsters never quit. Though around here, it could be a hobo." The bull took another drag off his stogie. "I'll call it in when I go back inside."

"No. You don't understand," Ron said. "He's a train passenger."

"Shit!" The bull pinched the ashes from his stogie and pushed it into his breast pocket. "Lead the way."

"Let's hurry," Ron said.

They raced down the tracks. It didn't take more than three minutes to reach the end of the yard and find the body.

"It looks untouched. I came out here and found the girl all messed up, with the two sailors rescuing her." Ron watched as the railway bull crouched beside the body and studied him. "Are you going to call it in? I need to freshen up and hopefully sleep a few winks, as I have a train to catch bright and early. What time is it?"

The railroad bull removed his watch, snapped the cover open and said, "Just after three. Go on. I'll call it in. What was the woman's name?"

"Good, thanks. Her name is Brita Torgerson."

"Your name again?"

"Ron Healy."

"I'll take over from here."

Ron raced back to the depot. The announcer's voice over the public address system drowned out all of his inner thoughts.

All aboard the two o'clock! Wichita, Topeka, and Santa Fe! ALLL ABOARD! Wichita, Topeka and Santa Fe! ALL ABOARD!

Passengers filled the many seats in the vast train reception room. A few were sound asleep and snoring, while others stared aimlessly ahead as if in a daze. Hats cocked sideways were almost slipping off the women's heads as they nuzzled against their husbands' shoulders. Men smoked cigars and let the thick smoke swirl up into the atmosphere. Burning cigarettes dangled from lips as ashes tilted downward like bent twigs. The smell of fresh strong coffee enveloped him.

Ron walked quickly toward the hotel stairs. His thoughts focused on the two young men who probably weren't old enough to drink anything stronger than grape Nehi, and it made him shudder. The idea of Brita being touched by the two young sailors who probably still read Lil' Abner comic strips made him angry.

*****

Immediately upon entering her room, Brita stripped off her clothes and dumped them in the garbage… but not before looking at the back of her skirt for any sign of blood. There wasn't any. She looked up toward the ceiling and said a silent prayer of thanks.

After shutting off the hot water and swirling up the suds, she climbed into the tub, lowered herself down, and immediately fell asleep.

Chapter Three

Day Two

The depot clock chimed five times when she stepped out of the water. Wrapping herself in a robe, Brita stretched and yawned, wandering over to look out the window at the silver Zephyr. The train was so very long that it stretched beyond her narrow window and back into the rest of the yard. The regular, boxy brown passenger trains looked like a set of children's toy blocks compared to the Zephyr.

She wondered if the victim from last night was Mr. Mindel. Could he be hidden somewhere inside, or was he shot? She breathed deeply.

The smell wafting up from her soiled clothes in the metal garbage bin assailed her senses. *The cattle yards are horrible smelling, and so is what's left of that outfit,* she thought to herself. After slipping into her clean uniform, the memories of the night before shattered her calm. Brita combed her hair and applied fresh lipstick, then looked over to the pile of clothes shoved into the bin again. She saw her rubber boots on the floor nearby. Before snapping her suitcase shut, she threw them in the trash on top of the ruined clothing.

She hadn't taken the time the night before to open her hollowed-out copy of *Gone with the Wind*. Opening it up, she sucked in her breath as a ripple of fear raced down her spine. The knife was gone. She hadn't been mistaken or delusional. The sight of the derringer made her feel a little bit better. Shivering, Brita reached for a blanket and drew it around her shoulders as she wondered about the knife. Her memory played over to when Ron appeared.

Brita placed the book inside of her suitcase and locked it shut. Anger welled up inside of her when she looked at the garbage bin. She threw off the blanket and blinked back tears. As she picked up her purse, she threw the bakery bag into the garbage. With the suitcase in hand, she marched out the door.

As she walked down the hallway toward the check-out desk, Brita's thoughts went immediately to the assault, which made her determined to go back to the scene. First on her agenda was to uncover facts if it was Mr. Mindel who was murdered, and then to locate her knife. Daddy would be horribly distraught if it went missing.

*****

Ron let out a yawn the size of Montana as he thought of Brita. When he looked in the mirror, he eyes were as red-lined as a roadmap. Ron quickly combed his hair, thinking of how beautiful Brita was, and how much he wanted to touch her.

He grabbed his bag and stepped out of the room. As Ron looked up the hallway, he couldn't miss the swing of Brita's hips and the sight of her long legs. It made him shake his head and mutter to himself, "Put her out of your mind. You value your fucking hands."

At the sound of a door closing, Brita stopped and glanced back.

"Good morning." Brita's gaze took in the full gist of him, her eyes growing wider with each of his approaching footsteps.

"Good morning to you, too. How did you sleep?" Ron couldn't pull his eyes away from her. Despite her obvious lack of sleep, her eyes still sparkled. The waves of curly hair showing from under her hat looked sexy.

"Lousy, but thanks for asking. I'm going out to the site," she answered, glancing at him. "I want to see it all for myself in the light of day. Then I'll know that it wasn't just a bad dream." She shivered. "By the way, how did you know my name last night?"

"Truthfully, I had heard you and the other Zephyrette,

Gladys, talking about pie and coffee… so I asked Gladys your name when I went searching for you. Last night I thought I had heard some shouting, but when I never heard another peep from your room…" He shrugged. "I just got worried. I asked at the main desk, and he told me your last name when I inquired if he'd seen you."

His answer was innocent and sincere. Brita finally said, "Okay, I believe you." She started walking again.

In unison, they handed their keys to the check-out clerk and walked away.

Ron urged her to hurry.

The public address system announcement shouted.

All aboard! Passengers travelling to Whiting, Gary, and South Bend. Alllll aaabooard!

They descended the hotel staircase, which brought them into the massive reception room. It was lined with people coming and going. Several people were sitting with luggage and waiting for their trains. Passengers formed a wall of traffic as Brita and Ron headed for the Zephyr.

"What did you find last night?" Brita asked. They wove through the passenger line to get to the right platform.

"Hold on… I wish the Z was closer," he replied. "I'll tell you about it in a few minutes."

Alllllll aboaaaaaaaaaaaaaard! All passengers leaving on the 8:14 Zephyr for Burlington, Omaha and Denver…Alllll aboooooooard!

When they reached the outside door, Ron said, "Remember we're in the Windy City."

"Yes, and soon rolling west to Denver."

Together they stepped out into the brisk early morning air. The fresh, crisp autumn wind took Brita's breath away, and she clutched her hat tight. Leaves crackled underfoot and swished around her bare ankles as the cold winds blew through the space between the trains.

"Here we are," Ron said.

Conductor Stan stood by the open door, and Brita was happy to see him. She gave him a big smile as he took her luggage and set it inside.

"Thanks."

"Heard there's been a murder and you were in the thick of it." Stan reached for Brita's hand and said, "The train departure may be delayed for a while because of the investigation. Don't worry about your duties just now. Gladys and I will settle the passengers."

"Thanks, I really appreciate this."

Stan finished helping Brita step into the train before turning to Ron. "Are you the new bartender?" he asked

"News travels fast," Ron said. He knew the general's staff was discreet, but it surprised him that Stan would know that he was the bartender. "Gladys tell you?"

"Of course! She's a rumor mill, Gladys. You catch on fast about who you want to tell anything to. I like that in an employee," Stan said with a grin.

"Figures. We'll take these to our rooms." Ron gave him a nod.

Ron steered Brita down the aisles and through the vestibules.

"This reminds me of the twenty-mile run that the soldiers do during basic training." When they reached their destination, she said, "I'm pooped."

The attendant stepped out to greet them. "I'm Dwight. If you need any help at all just let me know. Mr. Healy, I presume... and Miss Torgerson?" He raised a brow.

"Ron. I see that you've been informed of our arrival." Ron made another mental note about Gladys, the rumor mill. He thought that Dwight looked honest, despite his mysterious eyes.

"Yes. Stan, informed me of it. Brita, here's your room key, and Ron, here's yours. You two will serve the railroad well."

Dwight looked toward the opening vestibule door. "I have work to do." He headed toward the passenger car.

"We need to get outside," Ron said. They began walking away. "I'll tell you what I found the moment we step out the door."

"Good. I want to see everything in the daylight," Brita said. She opened her door, placed her suitcase inside, shut it, and turned the knob to make sure it was locked. "I'm set." She dropped the key into her pocket.

"Me too." His nose twitched and he stifled a sneeze.

They walked up the aisle and through the vestibule, giving Ron a few moments to collect his thoughts. The assailant could've left behind an article of clothing or a ticket stub near where he found Brita that could identify him. He also wondered about her knife.

At last they reached the crowded main door, but both chose to ignore the loading passengers.

"So here's the lounge car," Ron said. He grinned at the mirrored image of the bottles standing in a row. "Ready?"

Brita clutched her hat and cape tight as she stepped into the doorway. Ron placed his hand under her elbow. "Tell me what you found," she said.

"A body. The ticket stub said his name was Jacob Mindel."

"Oh no! I hoped it wasn't him. He was such a nice man. It makes me sick He was on the Twin Cities Zephyr."

"Did you know him very well?"

"Sort of, through Dad. He told anyone who asked that he was Norwegian and from Minnesota," she said. "He'd introduce himself as Mindelson, but his thick German accent would give him away. I'm sure he was worried that something might happen to him because he was Jewish. He was a scientist and defected to the US."

"Ever live in Germany?" Ron glanced at her. "I'm just wondering."

"My dad is a general, and we've lived in Germany. Schweinfurt, to be exact." Suddenly her head started to pound as sadness swept through her as she recalled seeing the figure strike the match and hearing the gunshot.

"Did you learn German?" Ron guided her around the trains and was happy that she let him help her step up and over the tracks.

"Yes. I became quite fluent." Brita asked, "I suppose all of the questions pertaining to Germany are because of the war?"

"Of course." Ron tried to sound nonchalant. "Do you happen to know Dr. Charlot Fortier?"

"Yes. He's my godfather and I've been told by my father that he's missing."

"Any ideas of where he might be found?"

"No." Brita shook her head. "Now that makes two, doesn't it?"

"Unfortunately, it does," Ron said.

"How do you know about Dr. Fortier?"

"I was told by someone last night after talking to the railroad bull," Ron said. "Are you sure that you're missing a knife?" Ron glanced at her. He couldn't figure out why the killer would take her knife, but not kill her. The whole incident was a mystery.

"Yes. I just checked my things, and it's not there. Maybe I dropped it. I hope that it's by the tree. At least that question would be answered. My father gave it to me for added protection." She stared up at the sky for a moment and shuddered.

As they walked, Ron wondered why her life had been spared, if someone else had seen the murder, and what had happened to her godfather, Fortier, and the knife.

"I see the police." Ron picked up his pace, urging Brita with a gentle pull of her arm. "I was out here quite a while searching the area."

"Sometimes I get dizzy from being tired and this place reeks from sewage," Brita said. "I might get sick again." She placed her hands inside of her pockets and clenched her hands into fists.

"Calm yourself. The police won't bite."

A whistle blew, and she jumped. The train became louder as it gained momentum. A boxcar full of coal swooshed past. The wind gust took her breath away. She clutched her uniform cape with one hand and hat with the other.

"The killer could've left me on the tracks," she murmured, more to herself than anyone else. The police were busy examining the body. Brita shivered.

"I forgot something," Ron said suddenly. "I'm going back to my compartment. You'll never know I've been gone."

"What? We just got here!" Startled, Brita grabbed his arm. "You can't go!"

"Just walk right up to them. I'll be right back." Ron raced away, leaving her alone.

"You'd better be." She sighed, watching him leave.

As she walked over to the police, she saw two cops talking, the railroad bull and some guys peering around a clump of trees, as well as several men who gathered around the victim. Brita couldn't take her eyes off the body; the unease that it caused brought tears to her eyes. If only she hadn't fallen, then maybe they both would've escaped unharmed. The two policemen saw her coming and shifted their gaze from the victim to her.

"Yes, ma'am?"

"I'm Brita Torgerson." She hoped that no one had contacted her father yet.

"Sergeant Poloski," he said, taking out his notepad. "I think you're just the lady we've been looking for." Poloski raised his arm and waved a uniform cop to come over. "He'll be right with you."

"Sure." Brita took the moment to catch her breath as she wondered why Ron had gone back to the train.

The police took notes as they milled around the body. Brita watched as they whispered back and forth, prodding and pointing at different parts of the victim.

"Ma'am?" the approaching policeman said. "May I get your

full name?" He opened his notepad and clicked his pen, holding it poised to write.

"Brita Torgerson." She watched him scribble.

"What did you see?"

"That's just it, I didn't see that much." She looked him in the eye. "I'm just really upset about this." She pinched her nose for a second. "It sure reeks out here."

"Agreed," he said. "It's been reported that you were hit over the head and knocked out. Tell me how you got into that situation. Start from the top, miss."

"I looked out my hotel window last night and saw two men. It looked as if one had a gun to the other's back." She shut her eyes to try and picture everything.

"Go on." He wrote down what she'd said. "You saw what you thought was a gunman…"

"Yes. I dressed and slipped out the door and went to locate the bull. He was busy, and I decided that he wouldn't believe me, so I tried to figure out where the two men went on my own. I found their footprints and followed," Brita said.

"Go on." He cleared his throat, and looked over to Sergeant Poloski.

"They spoke kind of loud, in German, but the noise of the stockyard, trains and the water muffled the sound. Then I saw a match light. I tripped and fell and must've made a noise, then I heard a gunshot."

"So you bumped your head when you fell?"

"No, the killer must have sneaked up on me and hit me from behind." She massaged her temples. "He gave me a pretty good-sized goose egg, too. He must have struck me pretty hard, because I was unconscious for a long time." Flexing her fist, she wanted to choke the assailant.

"Then what happened?"

"Huh? Oh…"

"What happened?"

"Two sailors found me."

"Do you remember their names?" He glanced down at his

notebook. She guessed he was reading the names, so when she reported them, he'd know if they matched.

"One was named Ax, the other, John. In fact, I was so mixed up, nervous, and scared that I'm not sure if I could tell you what they looked like. It was in the middle of the night, too." She hoped that she didn't sound too stupid.

"That's all right." He continued writing. "Then what?" He glanced over to Poloski, who was walking toward them.

"Let me see what you have, Officer, and I'll take over now." Poloski reached for the officer's notepad, and quickly perused it. "Good job. Now go back and keep watch, and for the love of God, keep the press away."

"Yes, sir." The uniform hiked back to the edge of the tracks and closer to where the horde of reporters would descend when they came.

"Tell me how you were able to see it," Sergeant Poloski said, his tone questioning, yet patient.

"I'm not exactly sure exactly where I was standing initially, because I moved and tripped." She began walking slowly toward the site. "It was very dark except for the moon and the yard lights."

"I see," Sergeant Poloski responded. "Do you know if anyone followed you? Did you see anyone besides the two men arguing?"

"No." She shook her head and thought for a moment. "I don't believe so. I don't remember seeing anyone else—except Ron, the bartender, who came as the sailors were reassuring me."

"Had you met the two sailors previously? Or Ron?" When she shook her head, he made another notation.

"Do you remember anything else?" He waited for her answer.

"I... I... don't really remember anything else." She scratched her head and sighed. "It's been a long night and morning. I didn't sleep, as you can imagine."

"We're almost finished. Did you know the victim?"

"Yes, and it's heartbreaking." Her heart beat so hard that she thought it would jump out of her chest.

"Tell me about him."

"He was a friend of our family's. A scientist. He and my father, General Torgerson, were friends. Dad knew he needed out of France, so he helped him get to Minneapolis. He was accompanying me here to Chicago, and told people his name was Mindelson and that he was Norwegian. He thought it would be a good disguise because of the war."

"How did Mindel act?"

"On the Twin Cities, he was fidgety, like he was nervous. But I don't know why." Brita wondered if she should mention her knife, then decided she'd better. "I had a small knife in my pocket, but now it's disappeared. I'm not sure what happened to it. Has anyone found it yet?"

"No…," Sergeant Poloski wrote what she'd said. "Hand knife, pocket knife? Anything distinguishable?"

"Army pocket knife from my dad."

"Okay." He wrote it down. "What did you do upon returning to the depot?"

"I bathed and went to bed." Brita suddenly yawned. "Excuse me." She felt that old blush returning again and wished that she could go to her room and then fall asleep for the next forty-eight hours. "Are you almost through with me?"

"Just about, but I want you stay on the train in case we need to ask more questions." He cleared his throat and reached into his uniform pocket and removed a picture. "Do you recognize anyone in this picture?" He held it up in front of her face, but wouldn't release it when she reached for it.

Brita studied it for a short moment. "The man on the right looks like Mindel. I don't recognize the other gentleman, but the writing on the ship is definitely not German or French."

"What language? Do you know?"

Brita thought. "It's Polish, I think."

"You can't be sure?"

"I'm just speculating, but I think it's a good guess."

"Thank you. You're free to go back to the train. I'll have a uniform walk you back."

"I'd like to look around for the knife, if you don't mind. It must be near where I fell." Her heart thumped as she waited for the answer.

"I want an officer with you," Poloski insisted.

"Thanks." Brita gave him a tentative smile. "You're not telling my father, are you?"

"No." He glanced at his notebook before leveling his eyes at her. "I'm leaving that up to your discretion."

"Thank you."

Sergeant Poloski motioned to the cop who'd initially interviewed Brita.

Brita poked through the leaves and around the roots with her foot before bending over and searching the site for at least a glint of the knife. She felt and touched patches of weeds and piles of leaves, but found nothing. She relived where she'd stood and distinguished which branch she'd tripped on, but closed her mind to the assault.

"I'm ready," Brita told the officer. She clutched her cape tighter and they began walking.

"This way," the officer said. "Are you holding anything back?" he asked. "Is there something that you're not telling us?"

"No. I'm upset. I knew the victim," she replied quickly. She looked away, and then back. "If I hadn't tripped, then maybe Mr. Mindel could've gotten away. Maybe I could've prevented the murder somehow. That's all." Brita sighed.

The officer steered Brita toward the main Zephyr door as they stepped over each track.

"You could have been killed. Next time, don't go following strange men in the middle of the night." The officer gave her a closer look. "I mean it. You could be killed."

The wind took her breath away as she brought her collar up higher against her neck.

The Zephyr's massive shovel front diesel electric engine

shone brighter than the morning sunshine. With the backdrop of orange maples and brown oak trees, the Zephyr looked like a thread of silver lace.

"Boy, she's beautiful… isn't she?" Brita murmured.

"You bet."

They walked up to the door where Stan stood greeting the passengers. The strength and warmth of Stan's hand wrapping around hers as she climbed inside gave Brita the assurance that no matter what, the train and its passengers were in good hands. Nothing on earth could go wrong because he was the protector — or so she hoped, and tried to convince herself.

"Good morning, again," Stan said. "Dwight informed me that your room door wasn't closed tight, Brita, so he took care of it."

"You're kidding me." Brita's breath caught in her throat. She wondered if Ron had returned to the train to snoop around her room? That was why he'd returned, she was positive.

Chapter Four

As Ron hurried back to the police, he'd hoped to meet with Brita, but wasn't able to. There were so many trains and corridors to walk that she could've been anywhere.

"Don't go any closer," a policeman hollered when Ron approached.

"I discovered the body," Ron replied. "I need to speak to your sergeant."

"Right over here, young man," Sergeant Poloski answered. He motioned to Ron. "Sergeant Poloski."

The railway bull glanced up from where he was looking. "Yep, he's the one." He straightened up and chewed on his cigar as he sized Ron up and down.

"Yes, I found the body," Ron said.

"Hold on a sec..." Poloski said, turning the page of his notepad. To the bull, he said, "We can take it from here." Poloski flipped through the pages of his notepad before turning to the bull, "Yep, they're on the Zephyr, heading for the West Coast. Take a look at their orders, would ya?"

"I'll get right on it." Plunging his thick hand in his bib pocket, the bull pulled out his gold watch and glanced at it before walking away.

"Let's move aside so that we can talk." Poloski tilted his head away from the body, and as they moved.

"I'm Captain Ron Healy and am working undercover as a bartender on the Zephyr," he said, showing it to the sergeant. "Please keep it under your hat."

"What?! You're an OSS agent working as a bartender?" Poloski frowned, then narrowed his eyes as he realized what Ron was telling him. "Explain yourself, Captain."

"My assignment is to keep the train safe. Brita doesn't know that her father issued my new orders. Naturally, he wants me to keep an eye on her as well." Ron shrugged.

"Hell of a night. Barely on the job and she almost got killed." Poloski shook his head and took in a deep breath. He put the notepad away and waited for Ron to begin. "Start from the top."

"It's puzzling." Ron frowned. He slid his badge back inside his wallet and put it away.

"Tell me how we got to where we are."

"When I checked in, I'd heard Brita and the other Zephyrette, Gladys, make arrangements to meet and have pie. When I found Gladys alone in the diner, I became suspicious."

"What time was that?"

"About midnight."

"Go on."

"I tried knocking, went to the front desk and had them buzz her room, and there wasn't an answer. I let myself into her room, and that's when I became quite worried."

"Why is that?" Poloski raised his brow.

"Everything seemed normal, but her purse was open and I looked inside and found her keys missing. Also, there was a chocolate roll, smashed, sitting beside it. It didn't add up. I've never heard of a woman going anywhere without her purse or skipping a chocolate roll." Ron shook his head, remembering. "I searched the depot, cafés and restrooms. At about one o'clock, I located the railway bull. He told me that a woman had passed by and then two sailors, walking the same direction."

"What did you see when you found them?"

"The sailors were drunk. They had a bottle of booze. One was trying to hold her upright, and the other was talking to her. But they said they were only trying to help her, and she verified that was the case."

"Then what?"

"She told me about she'd followed two other men. One of them lit a match, then she tripped and fell, and heard a gunshot.

Then somebody knocked her unconscious. Oh, and it seems that she lost her knife as well. Anyway, once she told me everything, she led me here, which took a little while because it was so dark and she was a bit disoriented. This brought us to about two or three o'clock. I had the boys walk her back, then I returned to the body."

"Okay. I'm set." Poloski took out the picture and said, "Recognize anyone?"

"Let me see…" Ron took it in his hands and studied it. "This guy is definitely our victim, and this other one looks so familiar." Ron scratched his head. He handed back the picture.

"Interesting." Poloski eyed the picture. "They're both nuclear scientists. This one," Poloski said, pointing at the picture, "is James Franck. He's my son's chemistry professor at the University of Chicago. Keep that under your hat." Poloski rubbed his chin. "Well, take a good look at the body, tell me if you see anything that might be of help to us. I've called in special agents. The train won't be leaving until all of our questions are answered or the murder is solved."

As they walked back to the body, Poloski scratched his whiskers. "I think I'll have a policeman watch Franck and his family for the next few weeks, just to be safe."

"Good idea." They stopped next to the body. "I can't tell you anything more, unfortunately."

"Too bad."

"Oh, there's one more thing," Poloski said.

"What's that?"

"An escaped Nazi prisoner was found trying to board a ship along the St. Lawrence Seaway. He was shot and killed while trying to run."

"Now we must be more cautious and on the lookout. Thanks for letting me know."

Poloski walked away while Ron stood over the body. He vowed to find the killer. He wondered if Brita was in any danger. The deeper he thought, the more perplexed he became.

"I've got to get back to the Zephyr," he told a nearby officer.

"If you need me, you know where to find me." Ron raced away.

*****

Brita quickly stepped inside of her room and shivered. The knowledge that someone may have searched her room gave her the jitters.

With her suitcase in hand, she marched out to locate Dwight and found him making another person's bed. Brita stood by the door.

"Dwight?"

"Yes, Brita." He finished smoothing the wrinkles out on the blanket.

"I want a different compartment." Her heart pounded, because she didn't feel safe anywhere.

"Why?"

"Because I just want a different one, that's all. Right next to the vestibule door, please." She gulped and felt her palms become sweaty.

"There's nothing wrong with the compartment. Why do you want another one?" Dwight waited patiently as she took a moment to gather her thoughts.

"Because of the door being ajar. I'd also like my name removed from the board, so that no one but you will know which compartment I have." She prayed that he'd grant her request.

"Ah. I understand now. I'll move you. Just so you know, those compartments can get drafty." Dwight studied Brita for a moment, then took her key, placed it on a hook, and removed a new one. "Follow me."

"Dwight, don't worry about me." She tried to assure him with a smile, but felt butterflies in her stomach.

Dwight led her down the corridor to compartment number one. "Here you are." He opened the door and handed the new key over. "I hope this will work out better for you. And I'll keep it our secret. If you have any trouble at all with anyone, just let me know. That's what I'm here for. If I can't solve it, then I'll bring it to Stan's attention. Okay?" He gave her a reassuring smile to make her feel more comfortable.

"Thank you. It's perfect. Now I can come and go quickly," she said. She tucked the key into her pocket.

"Our new passenger, Mr. Tennyson, can take your old compartment." Dwight's eyes twinkled as he nodded toward the new passenger approaching, then walked over and took the man's luggage.

Brita locked the door behind her and plunked down onto the bed. Yawning, she reached for a handkerchief to blow her nose. She was exhausted from lack of sleep, and her mind was muddled. She knew with certainty she had locked her door. Ron's excuse to return to the train was flimsy. She thought about the size of the gunman and compared him to Ron. She felt so mixed up. If only she could have heard what they'd said in German.

Pangs of guilt hit her and tears streamed down her cheeks. She wished that she could've saved Mr. Mindel from his horrible death.

Brita opened her suitcase and drew out a well-worn copy of *Gone With the Wind*. She opened it up to the hollowed-out section. She found her derringer still in its hiding place, then grimaced over the missing knife.

At the sound of a knock on the door, Brita quickly put the book back and snapped the suitcase shut and locked it.

"Brita! Open up! Quick. I have to speak to you. Hurry. Hurry!"

Suddenly wary, she wondered how Gladys already knew her compartment number. Brita took a deep breath and opened the door.

"Gladys."

"Can you believe it!" Gladys barged into the room. "A murder! Someone's dead and they think that the killer is on the train!" Gladys gushed, grabbing Brita's arm. "My goodness. It could be a passenger." She took a deep breath. "A murderer."

"Let's head to the lounge," Brita said, leading Gladys back

out the door. "Tell me all about it."

"A killer. Right amongst us. Can you believe it?"

"Settle down." Brita led her out into the vestibule and through the next car. "Don't worry, everything will be fine." Brita draped her arm around Gladys. "I'm sure of it."

"Oh my goodness, I thought it might have been you since you didn't meet me for pie last night. I was so scared, but I asked Dwight and he told me that you were alive. Thank goodness." Gladys took a moment to catch her breath. Her eyes opened wider. "Hurry up. We need protection. We can't be alone or we could be slashed to death. We can't defend ourselves against a cold-blooded murderer."

Window upon window lined their walk. Alongside the Zephyr were rows and rows of other trains. Some were boxcars transporting beef to points beyond from the stockyard next door. One train had cars full of coal and was heading west. The sight of the dingy brown coal cars was depressing and Brita couldn't wait to leave the station.

"I wonder when the train will get rolling?"

"Don't worry, Gladys. We'll know soon enough." She tried to calm her friend, but wondered the same thing herself.

They walked through several cars until they entered the lounge. Ron stood behind the bar, and it made her feel unsettled.

"What happened to Billy? Why isn't he the bartender?" Gladys asked Ron.

"Yes. Tell us about yourself, please," Brita said. Brita gave him a cold look as she tapped her fingers on the counter.

"Ron. Just Ron. I'm the new bartender, and I don't know what happened to Billy." Ron gave Brita a questioning look.

"Just Ron, how long have you been a bartender?" Brita drummed her fingers. "Is this your first job?" With a blank look, she stared at him.

"Excuse me ladies, but I have work to do," he replied. A customer was approaching, and he put on a smile.

Stan walked into the dining car and raised the microphone

to speak into.

Well, folks! The grand silver Zephyr is now boarding. It's time to get rolling, I've been told! Alllllllll abooooooard!

"Time for us to get to work," Gladys said, jamming her elbow into Brita's side. "It's your turn to show the passengers where to go. I'm staying in the dining car."

"Okay, I'll head toward the passenger cars." Brita figured that she'd soon be crippled from Gladys' elbow bashing. She quickly walked away.

Mr. and Mrs. Magnusson from the Twin Cities Zephyr entered with their suitcases, and Brita walked over to them.

"May I help you?" Brita asked. "Let me carry your luggage." She reached for the handbag.

"Take us to the porter, would you please?" Mr. Magnusson requested.

"Right this way." She quickly scanned the ticket to find out where to go.

As they walked through the first two coaches, Brita was relieved that neither passenger said anything about the murder. She hoped that no one knew about it, because false rumors would make everyone uneasy.

"How many more cars do we have to walk through?" Mrs. Magnusson said, trying to catch her breath. Her hat feather bobbed up and down, and she clutched the railing whenever possible.

"Only a few," Brita replied. She glanced down to Mrs. Magnusson's feet and discovered the reason behind the woman's reluctance to walk. She wore high-heeled shoes with sharp pointed toes. Brita hoped Dwight wasn't busy so that he could immediately help them. "You two were on the Twin Cities Zephyr, weren't you?"

"Yes. Our good friends, the Bakkos, were there also. They should've boarded by now. We're traveling together."

"Here we are, the final car." She was happy, because

walking through five cars was a long walk. "Dwight will be right with you." She looked up and noticed him peek out from a room. "Enjoy your ride."

Brita headed back to the lounge. As she entered the vestibule, another set of passengers was passing through.

"Does anyone need help?"

When no one answered, she headed toward another coach.

Mounds and mounds of coal rolled past her window, and the whoosh of wind caused by a passing train rattled the windows. On the heel of the caboose, there was sunshine. Leaves flew in the air and feathered down to the earth like a symphony.

Once she'd made it back inside the sixty-four passenger seat car, a gentleman reached out and grabbed her hand.

"Yes, sir?" She looked down at him. "How may I help you?" She pulled her hand back.

"I'd like a newspaper if you don't mind, miss. I don't see one anywhere." He raised his eyes to her and removed his fedora, revealing beady brown eyes and a broad forehead.

"I'll see if I can find one," she replied. "What is your name?"

"Smith."

Brita walked away, shivering as she kept reciting his name. His name couldn't be Smith, she reasoned. He looked like Al Capone's brother, which made her think that people really weren't who they seemed to be at times. She found the paper and casually slid it into his lap, then walked away.

Voices of passengers echoed loudly before she opened the lounge door. Smoke filled the room, turning it blue. She looked toward a few booths where men chewed on cigars or smoked cigarettes. Most held cards in their beefy fists. Off in the far corner, Brita noticed two passengers from the Twin Cities Zephyr, Carlo and Jacques, who were busy rolling dice. She grinned as Carlo spilled the dice across the counter top and a passing train's reverberation made them slide to the floor.

"Brita!" Carlo held up his empty bottle. "How about bringing us another round? Ron will put it on our bill." He winked at Brita and grinned as she blushed.

"Sure." Brita turned to Ron, who already had the drinks ready. With the cold bottles in hand, she went back to the men.

"Here you are." She set them down and glanced at Carlo. He looked tired, and his clothes were rumpled. She decided that he must be losing the most money.

"Thanks." Jacques took his and immediately took a drink. "You sure are pretty." He chuckled as he was rewarded when Brita's cheeks lit up like cherries.

"Thank you." Brita quickly walked away and hoped that no one else saw her blushing.

From a distance, she tried to watch as Ron poured drinks and served beer. The night before seemed like more than just a few hours ago. When he'd rescued her, his hands had felt strong and his baritone voice had resonated in her ears, sounding magical. Now she noticed how his soft brown hair flopped about like a little boy's. She thought his eyes looked mysterious, like they were hiding dark secrets.

The outside door burst open, bringing with it a brisk wind. Two men wearing long wool coats and carrying briefcases entered. Stan was right behind them.

"This way, sirs," Stan said. He steered them toward the vestibule.

Brita watched them walk away. A young woman holding a child nudged her.

"Would you please help me? I can't find the correct car."

"Follow me," Brita said after reading her ticket.

Brita carried her suitcase as they walked through several coaches.

"It feels cold out there," Brita said.

"It's only about thirty-five degrees."

Brita guided her through to the women's coach, where they had more privacy.

"Here you are. Enjoy the trip."

"Do you help us with the children?" a different woman asked. "My name is Molly."

"Whenever I can." Brita smiled at her. "I'll be back, I still have passengers to check in."

As she walked, Brita noticed all the full seats. Smoke lingered in the air.

Brita passed Mr. Smith and still wondered if he was a gangster. She walked swiftly to the observation deck, which took her through the sleeping cars and two other cars. She'd timed herself, and found that it took a good twenty minutes to walk from the lounge to the observation deck coach, plus climbing the stairs. Once on the top of the stairs, she was astounded by the panoramic view. Even in the railyard, the passengers could still see for miles out into the town, or off to the west to see open farmland. It was breathtaking.

Toward the front, she thought she recognized two of the sailors sitting near some marines. She walked over to them.

"Ax?" she said after clearing her throat.

"Well now, if it isn't the damsel in distress," John said. He gave her a smile. "You're prettier in the daylight hours."

"I think so too." Ax gave her a grin. "You're looking good. How about a date?"

"Not right now, thanks, but, if you need anything at all, just let me know." Brita gave them each a nod and a smile. "Have the police questioned you yet?"

"Not yet, toots," Ax said.

Brita nodded and headed toward the back of the room. As she descended the stairs, the announcement crackled overhead. She stopped to listen.

All Burlington personnel are to meet in the dining car!

As Brita passed through the passenger car, she noticed a middle-aged lady with a knitting basket on the floor and a bag on her lap. She held a Cracker Jack toy beside her ear and was snapping it. Brita chuckled to herself, because the small metal object was the size of a cricket and sounded like one too, which made the woman look silly. In another seat sat a woman with too much pink rouge on her cheeks, and she was applying more. Brita was sure that she'd been on the Twin Cities Z, because she remembered the lady's super bright red lipstick.

Stan announced…

Burlington personnel to the dining car, immediately!

Brita picked up her pace. The twenty-minute walk seemed like an eternity. Finally, she entered the lounge. She noticed Ron was already in the dining car as she passed through.

Voices echoed as she opened the dining car door and stepped inside. Stan motioned to an empty chair right beside Dwight. She gladly took it.

"Now that we're all finally here," Stan began, looking at Brita. "I have news to share." He cleared his throat to get everyone's attention. "There was a murder last night in the rail yard, which needs further investigation. On board are two OSS agents to question passengers and personnel." He took a moment to study the people gathered. "You're to comfort the passengers in any way possible. I'm sure that it will be resolved soon. Any questions before we get started?"

"Will the train be delayed long?" Ron asked. He crossed his arms and appeared anxious as he waited for the answer. He also didn't know about the agents.

"I'm not sure, but I'll keep everyone updated." Stan took a look around the room. "Any more questions?"

"Was it a passenger that was murdered?" Gladys asked.

"The little that I know, I can't tell you. That's the way it is, sorry," Stan answered. "When I learn anything that I can pass along, I will let you all know."

Brita glanced over at Gladys and realized that the room was full of people she didn't know.

"Yes. But we are in Chicago, where murders happen all the time. It could've been done by a hobo, also." A few people nodded in agreement when Harold, the dining car porter, spoke up as he glanced around the room.

"I bet you're right," another porter said, crossing his arms.

"There have been escaped prisoners of war," Ron said.

Brita shifted in her seat and tightened her fists. She wanted to scream and shout and let everyone know the sort of person the killer truly was. She drew in a deep breath and stared out of the window.

"Why have OSS agents been called in to investigate?" Gladys asked. She smiled from ear to ear as the room hushed.

"Truthfully, Gladys, I don't know," Stan said, he shook his head. "As I said, when I know something, I'll keep you all informed." Stan took stock of the employees and hoped that he'd satisfied their curiosity.

If Gladys knew what had really happened, she'd be hysterical, Brita thought, shuddering.

"Any more questions?" Stan asked. Taking out his railroad watch, he took a quick look. "Time to get back to work. I want all of you just to continue about your business. If anyone asks about a murder or when the train will start rolling, just tell them the truth—and the truth is that you don't know anything." He slipped the watch back inside of his pocket. "Brita. Come with me."

Brita had known that she'd be the first questioned and had readied herself for the ordeal. As she walked out of the room, she felt all eyes watching her.

"They want to interview the two sailors first. Do you know where they are?"

"Yes. They're in the observation deck. Do you want me to point them out to you?"

"Yes. You seem a little nervous," Stan said. He placed his hand on her arm. "This is all routine. Don't worry. It will clear up in no time at all, mark my words." He gave her a serious look.

"You're right. You're absolutely correct." She gave him a tentative smile as they walked.

A train rushed by beside them, clearing the way for sunshine and a view of the street, where children played hopscotch and kick the can. Cars lined up to drop off passengers and pick them up. Brita noticed that the car fumes hung in the air from the cold.

As they crossed through the passenger car, Brita noticed that the lady with the Cracker Jack toy was now knitting, and the bag was on the floor. The young woman with the heavy makeup was reading.

"This is a long walk," Brita mentioned.

"Yes, it is. But after doing it for a day or two, it'll go fast and you won't notice it." Stan tried to reassure her. As they continued, he said, "There's a war happening. That must explain why the police are being more cautious, questioning every potential witness or suspect thoroughly. We just passed the compartment that the two agents are in."

"I see they're near my compartment. Please don't tell where it is. Just you and Dwight know for the time being, but somehow Gladys discovered it." Somehow, it gave Brita comfort.

"There's Gladys for you."

"Yes. She knows everything about everyone."

When they approached the vestibule, another train whizzed beside them. Brita caught herself clutching the railing tight because the compressed air rattled and shook the car.

"I always enjoy the view from the observation deck." Stan held the handrail and waited for Brita to start climbing the stairs.

"Me, too." Brita started up. "Should I just point to them?" She was hesitant, not knowing what to do.

"Yes."

They briefly stared out to the distant north, noticing the canals as they angled and curved from the Chicago, Des Plaines, and Illinois rivers, which carried the sewage to the Mississippi River. Train trestles carried passengers over the canals.

Brita turned her attention to the front of the deck where the large windows were, and saw the servicemen lined with a cigarette hanging from their mouth or fingers.

"The two on the right, third row," she said.

"Thanks. You can go back to work now."

Brita quickly descended the stairs. The fresh air between the cars helped to clear her mind.

*****

As Ron walked back to the lounge, he mulled over the picture Sergeant Poloski had shown him. He wondered where the photo was taken, and by whom. As he looked out the window, he noticed the railroad bull walking toward the depot. Poloski was just stepping out of the depot and called the bull over. Ron wondered when he'd be called for questioning.

Ron glanced up and noticed a passenger coming toward him.

"Got a Schell's? I'm thirsty. Name's Swensen," he said. "What's your handle?"

"Ron." Ron reached for the bottle of Schell's and opened it. "There you are."

"How come we're still sittin' here?" Swensen took a quick swallow. "What's the poop, I mean scoop?" He glanced up at Ron.

"What do ya mean?" Ron looked at him, then shifted his gaze to an approaching customer. "What'll ya have?"

"Gin and tonic for me, and a brandy Manhattan for my buddy, Jacques." He took a cigarette and lit it up as he waited. "Name's Carlo."

"Coming right up, Carlo," Ron said, and quickly mixed their drinks. "There you are." He set them in front of his customer, happy that they didn't ask for anything more complicated.

"Thanks."

"How's your luck going with the dice? Used to do that years ago," Ron asked, making conversation.

"Not too shabby. This round's on Jacques," he said, rolling the cigarette in his mouth. After taking a slight sip, he said, "Good," before carrying the drinks to his partner.

Ron grinned and almost wished that he could join them, just for some fun. He started to wipe the counter.

"You from around here?" Swensen drank his beer, then lit a cigarette.

"Nope. Where you from?"

"Minneapolis. I saw the Marx Brothers at the Orpheum Theater and some other vaudeville acts. Sure was fun. Had this dame with me who was... well... a hot tomato." He blew smoke in the air. "Got a dame?"

"Nope." Ron wished that this guy would leave; he was nosy and kept talking, and Ron wasn't in any mood to be around people at the moment. *Wouldn't make a very good real bartender,* he thought sheepishly. He was worried about Brita and how the investigation was going. Relief spread through him when Swensen suddenly snuffed out his cigarette and walked away.

Ron took a moment to glance out the window again while drying glasses and saw Poloski striding toward the train door. He stopped for a moment to speak with another policeman. The two entered, and the policeman headed toward another car as Poloski walked over to Ron.

"How's it going?" Poloski asked, placing his elbow down on the counter. He studied Ron for a moment. "How reliable is..." He paused and removed his notepad from his pocket. "Gladys?"

"I don't know. The first time I saw her was last night, but I'd bet my ass that she's a gossip. That's my one and only impression."

"Thanks for the honesty." Poloski flipped his notepad shut and shoved it into his pocket. "Where might I find her?"

"I'm not sure. The last time that I saw her, she was heading toward the women's lounge car." Ron looked up as a passenger approached the bar. "What would you like?"

"How about two seven-ups for the ladies, and two beers?"

"Coming right up," Ron replied. He reached for the bottles, uncapped them and handed them over. "That'll be seventy cents."

"Here you are," the man responded, placing the coins down. He picked up the bottles and walked away.

Ron turned his attention back to Poloski.

"If you see Gladys, keep her occupied for me, will you?" Poloski asked. "I'm going to start walking, and if I don't run into her shortly, I'll be back."

"Will do."

Ron watched him walk away.

The room was filling up with more men and rough voices. Blue ribbons of smoke hung in the air. Poker games had begun, and chips were flying. As he looked around the room, he noticed that the men who had purchased the beers and sodas were in a booth, and they held cards their hands. Jacques and Carlo were busy drinking and rattling dice. Ron suspected that they'd be after girls before the night arrived.

Another swoosh from a passing train caught him off guard as the Zephyr seemed to shake from a wall of wind streaming past. Ron was sure that it wouldn't be long before another train filled that vacancy.

Another announcement roared overhead.

Gladys Muldoon is wanted in the lounge car as soon as possible.

In a few short moments, Poloski re-entered the lounge and stood by the doorway. He took out his watch and glanced at it, frowning.

Ron looked at his and noticed that it was already noon, and time for lunch.

A poker playing customer raised his hand and hollered, "Bring another round of drinks and beers and put it on my tab—Jim."

"Coming right up." Ron poured and mixed the drinks, opened two bottles of beer, and set everything on a tray.

"Here you are, Jim," he said as he placed the drinks down.

When Ron returned to the bar, he noticed that Gladys had entered and was standing beside Poloski. He couldn't keep his eyes from watching Gladys. She shifted from one foot to the next as Poloski wrote notes. She crossed and uncrossed her arms and scratched her head. When Poloski was writing and she wasn't talking, she was looking all around the room. Raking her fingers through her hair caused some of her Victory rolled hairdo to fall down. She moistened her fingers with her lips and brought the hair back up, repositioning the hairpin. When she started walking toward Ron, he knew that he'd be in for an earful.

"Can you believe it?" she asked, still half way across the room.

"What's that?" Ron could barely hear her over the din of the voices and clanging of a nearby intersection bell.

"I swear he thinks that I did it." She crossed her arms, clamped her jaw tight, and nodded.

"I'm sure you're getting upset over nothing. What did they ask?" Ron asked, trying to calm her down.

"All sorts of questions." She took a deep breath. "He wanted to know what I did last night. Where I went. Did I see anyone that I knew? What I ate. When I got back to the room. What time for this or that… I'm never asking anyone to join me for pie and coffee ever again. That much I can tell you for sure." She shook her head. "Being friendly just causes problems. It's not worth it. Now they think that I did it."

"I don't think that you have anything to be concerned about." He stood up when he noticed that another customer was coming over. "You'll be fine."

"Thanks a lot, partner." Gladys took a deep breath and headed toward the vestibule.

Ron noticed that Poloski had left the room and presumed he was taking his notes to the agents. After they'd reviewed the notes, he was sure it would be his turn to be questioned. He wondered how Brita had held up, or if she had even been interviewed yet.

Chapter Five

When Brita passed the compartment where the agents were, she shuddered. In her mind, she pictured Mindel and felt miserable, renewing her vow to bring the perpetrator to justice. She quickened her pace as she walked from one car to the next.

School bells rang in the distance. Glancing outside, she noticed children rush outside for recess. As she stepped through the vestibule, she looked toward the seat where two women were sitting. The woman with the heavy makeup was still reading her book. Brita walked over toward her.

"My name's Brita. Good book? I've wondered if I should read it or not."

"Rose Olson. I absolutely love *Gone With the Wind*. Rhett Butler is so handsome. Scarlett is like her name… brazen." She marked the page and closed the book. "Have a seat."

"You were on the Twin Cities Z too, weren't you?" Brita sat down beside her. "I feel like I recognize you."

"You brought me tea."

"Oh, yes, now I remember," Brita said, feeling a little foolish. She told herself that no one could possibly remember all the people from one train to the next.

"By the way, what can you tell me about the murder? There are rumors flying all over about it," Rose said. She placed her hands on top of the book. "Tell me, will you? I'm a little frightened since I'm traveling all the way to Denver. What if the killer is a passenger?" She studied Brita.

"I wouldn't worry about it." Brita shivered. It was on her mind too, and frightening. "I do know that there are two OSS agents investigating, and I think it's because it was in the rail yard and not on the street. This is the home of Al Capone, remember." Brita wondered, knowing since her life was at stake.

Stan's voice blared again on the overhead system.

Will Brita Torgerson please come to car number five as soon as possible.

"It's been a pleasure." Brita stood up. "I must get back to work."

"Let me know if you learn anything more." Rose removed her makeup compact and began to reapply her lipstick as Brita walked away.

Brita's anxiety and frustration returned. Her temples throbbed with worry. As she hiked from one car to the next, she rehearsed over and over what had happened the night before. By the time that she came to the doorway, her nerves were once again frayed. She took a deep breath and knocked.

The door opened, and she heard someone say her name.

"Yes. Brita Torgerson." She looked into the deep-set brown eyes of a man who reminded her of a bean pole wearing a dark suit. His navy bow tie and pressed white shirt were impeccable. His handshake was firm, reminding her of her dad, and she relaxed for the moment.

"I'm Agent Lund, and this is Strand." He motioned for her to sit down.

"Brita, have a seat," Agent Strand said. He gave her a nervous smile. His nod toward the opposite bench caused Brita to wonder if this was his first case. He waited to continue until she'd sat. "Let's get started. Tell me what happened last night, please."

"Start from when you checked in," Agent Lund said, poising his pen. "Harold should be bringing tea."

Just as he spoke, there was a knock on the door.

"Come in."

All three looked toward the door as it opened.

"Here is your tea," Harold said. He carried in a tray with

cups, a teapot, and a couple slices of lemon on a small plate. "I'll be back to collect them later. Can I get you anything else?" He glanced from agent to agent while pouring tea in all three cups.

"No, thank you," Agent Strand answered coolly, and cleared his throat.

Harold disappeared out the door.

"Let's begin," Agent Strand said, and reached for his cup.

Brita recounted the previous night's events to the two agents, starting from the time she checked in and noticed Ron. She admitted to herself how handsome he'd looked. She explained the prearranged meeting with Gladys for pie and coffee. Continuing, she described the scene she'd witnessed looking out her window, and why she went in search of Mr. Mindel.

Her face grew paler and her heart beat faster as she got closer to describing the details of the murder. She told about seeing the lit match, falling down, and hearing the gunshot. She also described when she woke up. She tried to remember what she'd heard, but the voices had been too muffled. Then she explained about the sailors and Ron, and how he had located the body.

Her heart had thumped through it all, and when she'd finished, Brita noticed that she'd wrapped her knuckles around the bench edge and her palms were wet from sweat.

"You didn't understand what was said, did you?"

"No, not really," she said, shaking her head. "Also, the knife that I'm missing is from my dad." She took a deep breath, and said, "I hope it's found."

"We'll do our best."

"Thanks. You've been very helpful." Agent Strand shoved the pencil behind his ear and rubbed his eyes. "You may go now."

Brita walked out. Tension began to flow from her body now that her turn was over. She wondered when they'd be through questioning, and if they'd find out who did it.

*****

Ron checked his watch when Brita was summoned, and it had been around two. He worried about her. It had been really busy at the bar, and since he wasn't a bartender by trade, keeping up with the drinks and beers had been a challenge. Fortunately, the orders had died down with the lunch hour. He looked up as Stan entered the car.

"Brita is finished, and you're next," Stan told him. "Do you know which compartment they're in?"

"No." Ron shook his head.

"Number five, two cars down." He took out his watch and said, "Already close to two-thirty. I can't believe it. Before you know it, they'll be having us take the luggage out because we'll be here overnight."

"Ever happen before?"

"Nope. Harold is here now, he'll relieve you." Stan turned and walked away.

"Here." Ron handed Harold the bar towel. "Have fun. I'll be back when I can."

"Just what I need to do, be a bartender. I hope they all want beer or grape Nehi."

Ron chuckled as he walked away, glad to get away from all the questions and rumors floating throughout the train.

Passing through the vestibule, Ron's wondered how it went for Brita.

The buzz of activity in the large passenger coach echoed in his ears as he strode down the aisle. When he reached the end, an elderly man grabbed his arm.

"Sonny?"

"Yes?" Ron said, stopping.

"Help me to my room please, sonny. My back's acting up." He started to push himself out of his seat, but plunked back down again. "Damn! You want some advice, don't live to get old."

"Ah… sure." Ron placed his arm under the man's arm and

raised him up. "Let's go. Where are you headed?"

"Compartment three, the next car," he said. The man used Ron as a support.

"It's right where I'm going," Ron said. He led the man down the aisle and opened and closed the doors as they passed through the vestibule.

"Would you help me inside?" the man said.

Ron opened the door and let it shut as he helped the man sit. "Are you set? Do you need any more help?" He stood with his hand on the doorknob.

"Go ahead. Thanks a lot." He breathed heavily, as if he'd just run a marathon.

"Any time."

Ron stepped out of the door, only to see Brita coming toward him.

"Hello," Ron greeted her. "How are you doing?"

"Okay," Brita's eyes narrowed as she studied him for a short moment.

Brita rubbed her chin as she walked away.

*****

When Ron entered compartment five, he was wondering why Brita seemed so distant.

"Have a seat, Captain," the two agents said in unison.

"I'm Agent Lund, and this is Strand. I must admit, your employment status is pretty impressive, Captain. You've done a fine job for the security of our country."

"Thank you." Ron felt better knowing that they'd done their job and looked into his record. "Any clues yet?"

"Ever see this guy before?" Agent Lund showed him a different picture, one he hadn't seen before.

"Sergeant Poloski asked the same question about a different picture. Obviously Mindel's on the right, but the other guy... no. However, it may be that he's Charlot Fortier. I'm not sure. Brita's father helped Mindel and a Charlot Fortier escape the Nazis." Ron sat back in the bench and wondered what was coming next.

"Who's this Fortier?"

"A missing mathematician from Paris."

"I'll check into that. Anything else about him?"

"No." Ron shook his head.

"It's seems that this Mindel is the third Jewish scientist to have been murdered in the last three weeks."

"You're kidding, right?" Ron sat upright and stared at the two men. "Are they connected?"

"You mean the murders?" Agent Strand said. He jutted out his chin and massaged it. "We don't really know for sure. It's hard to find out much about either of them."

"Take a look at this tie and belt. It was found near the body." Agent Lund held it up for Ron to view.

"It's tied with an odd knot," Ron replied, studying it. "You'd think it would've been a Windsor, but it's not."

"Know anything about Brita's knife?"

"Not at all. It must've fallen out of her pocket."

"Do you have anything else at all to add?" Agent Strand peered at him over the rim of his teacup. He took a swallow and winced. "Cold already."

"Do you think the killer is a passenger?" Ron scratched the back of his head before yawning. "Sorry, it's been a long day already."

"I don't think it was a passenger. I suspect you haven't had much sleep." Agent Lund hesitated but finally said, "There have been several suspicious inquiries as to when the train would be arriving from Minneapolis. So that makes me think that it's not a passenger."

"That's a relief, but the inquiries could've been from the general lining up my assignment," Ron said.

"Didn't consider it, but you may be on to something. Now give me a rundown again of what happened." Agent Lund lifted his notebook, ready to write with poised pen.

"Sure." Ron recited the story once again. When he finished, he asked, "Was there anything found on Mindel that I may not be aware of? I did search the body, but didn't find any hidden messages or weapons. Also, I'd like to know what his schedule was." Ron didn't hear anything unusual or different from what he already knew except that there were three long distance phone calls made verifying the Zephyr's schedule from the Twin Cities to Chicago and then on to Denver. "Thank you," Ron said, and stood up. "It's time for me to get back to work."

"If you see or hear anything, please let our office know about it once you reach Burlington, Iowa."

"Of course. I haven't had a chance to send a telegram to the general, either. I think that I should do that now."

"As you wish. We'll be wrapping up our investigation soon. We're fairly sure that the killer is still in Chicago, and that Brita's role was coincidental. We have to study our notes before giving a final departure time."

"I understand."

Ron stepped of the Zephyr and out into the late afternoon sunshine, drawing in a deep breath. The crisp air and strong winds seemed to clear his head, and he felt better. As he walked into the depot, his thoughts went to what the agents had told him. Three murdered scientists—how odd. He also wondered about the tie's knot.

The main lobby was filled with waiting passengers. The overhead public address system crackled.

All aboooooooooooooooard! All Burlington passengers to Topeka and points beyond! Alllllllll abooooooooooard on platform nine! Allllllllll passengers traveling the Twin Cities Zephyr are to load on track number five. Allllllll Abooooooooard!

Ron marched straight toward the Western Union office, tapped on the door and went inside.

"I need to send a telegram. How soon can it get out?" he asked. Ron noticed how clean and neat the office was. The man's pitch black skin contrasted against his white shirt, but his black shirt cuffs kept the ink from staining his shirt. His bright smile was welcoming.

"Right away. Just write it out." He handed Ron a slip of paper, a pen and ink jar.

Ron wrote: Suspect yard murder STOP. Bird's fine STOP. Arrange BI briefing STOP. C.R.H.

"Here," Ron said, handing over the message.

"It'll go right out."

"Thanks."

Ron felt better knowing that the general would be kept informed. When the train reached Burlington, Iowa, Ron hoped that the agents would have more information about Dr. Fortier and this murder.

Threatening clouds covered the sunshine as he stepped outside.

When he entered the train, he realized that the staff had been notified that the train would soon be departing. He noticed Brita trying to calm an older woman.

Ron took a moment and tried to summon the image of his former fiancée, Margot, but couldn't. It angered him, because he just might be on the trail of her killer.

Stan's voice echoed loudly overhead.

"May I have your attention, please? Dinner is now served in the dining car. Because of the delay, all beverages will be on the house for the next hour. I hope that you'll enjoy your extra time. We will head for Burlington just as soon as we get the go-ahead. Over and out."

Brita had spent hours walking back and forth and seeing to customers' needs. She stopped for a moment and looked at Dwight.

"Do you have a list of the passengers from the Twin Cities Z that are on the coach?" She'd decided to do a little investigating on her own, since it sounded as if the train would be soon leaving Chicago. She might never learn who was responsible, which was bothersome.

"Why?" Dwight asked, writing down the name of the

passenger he'd just brought fresh water.

"I'm just curious… I'd like to refresh my memory with the names and so on… you know, so that I don't have such a time with it." She hoped that her excuse would satisfy his curiosity.

"Well, okay. You seem to be coping well after the ordeal… not like nervous Gladys, who is chirping about," he said. Dwight reached for the list and gave it to her. "Put it back when you're finished. I've got work to do." He began to walk away.

"Thank you," she said. Brita gave him a tentative smile. "I appreciate this." She quickly grabbed a sheet of paper and wrote the names and compartment numbers down, stuffing it into her pocket.

The intercom announcer spoke once again.

We have been given the go-ahead for the final boarding call and departure. Alllllllllll abooooooooooooooard!

Brita immediately walked away toward the main entrance to assist the passengers who had been on the Twin Cities Zephyr, or hadn't been able to board because of the murder investigation.

Brita glanced out and saw the clock tower as it readied to chime five o'clock. The steepled roofs and the great clock tower reminded her of a medieval castle.

At last she made it to the lounge car where Gladys was already greeting people.

"Good afternoon," Brita said. She nodded to the many passengers.

Businessmen wearing bowler hats entered and went to sit in the lounge chairs. One man lit up a cigar. Four others gathered around a table, and one removed a deck of cards from his inside breast pocket.

Women with hair done up in pompadours or curls wore brightly colored fall dresses, seamed silk stockings, and shiny shoes, heading toward the other coaches.

"Welcome aboard, I'm Brita, she said to a young mother

stepping past her. "If I can be of service, just let me know."

"Thanks, I'm Annie." The young woman held a baby. "Can you tell me where my compartment is located, please? I'm a little nervous." Her eyes shone bright as she held the sleeping baby in one arm and the diaper bag and satchel in the other.

"I'll take you to it."

"Thanks."

"Let me carry something," Brita said. She took the satchel and diaper bag and led Annie to her compartment after looking at the passenger roster.

Brita's legs ached as she carried suitcase after suitcase down the train's corridor. When everyone seemed situated and satisfied, she glanced at her watch. It was seven o'clock. Her muscles and feet hurt, and she wondered if she'd get gorilla muscles from all of the lifting.

"Ma'am." A priest lifted his hat to greet her in the corridor.

"Good day, Father…?"

"O'Malley," he replied.

"Father O'Malley." Brita kept walking toward the lounge car.

Passengers had started playing cards. Feathered hats bobbed while women knitted or crocheted projects as they visited. Men studied the newspaper, folding and unfolding them while anxiously looking outside. The voices carried through into the vestibule.

The next car was full of mothers and children. She gave a nod to Annie, who was busy talking with a fellow passenger.

As Brita walked, she grew more and more determined to find out exactly why Ron had left her this morning instead of accompanying her to the police. She also wanted to know why she saw him leave the other room as she left the compartment with the two OSS officers. He wasn't an attendant, so he shouldn't have been there. There also was the matter of her room door being found open after she'd just locked it. It all added up to one big question mark.

Smoke hung in the air, and the noise of the card players and observers hit her like a wall. Men were standing or sitting with suitcases, and women stood with hands on hips as they looked on. Ron was behind the bar and serving drinks. She strolled over to him.

Ron grinned. When she rested an arm on the bar, he raised his finger to her and said, "Just a minute." He finished serving two beers to a suited gentleman and took the money. "Thanks."

"Anytime." The gentleman took the beers and walked away.

"Do you have a minute?" Brita stared into his brown eyes. She looked at his full, floppy hair and his appealing mouth, and tried to convince herself that he was just like any other handsome man.

"For you? Sure. Anytime." He scratched his chin. "How did the questioning go?"

"Just fine, but that's not what's bothering me." She gave him a slight smile, and felt the darn blush coming to her cheeks. "Why did you turn around and go back to the train instead of walking with me to the police?"

"I thought I had recognized someone, but I was wrong. The person has always been on my radar as not very likeable so I wanted to make sure that it wasn't him." Now that she'd finally asked what was bothering her, Ron let out a sigh of relief, even though she still had the look of suspicion on her face. "Is that all?"

"What were you doing in a passenger's compartment when I came out of questioning?" She tried to sense or read deception in his eyes.

"I had just been summoned for questioning. An elderly man needed help walking, and he enlisted me. It's that simple… you can go ask him." He shrugged and gave her a smile. "Is that all? Are you satisfied now?"

"Answer me one question… if it wasn't you, then who opened my locked room door? They probably went through my things, too." She stared at him with wide opened eyes. "I need to know." She crossed her arms and clamped her jaw tight.

"What?" Ron's heart jumped to his throat. He could barely breathe as he stared at her. "When did that happen?" When she wouldn't tell him, Ron reached out for her arm. "When? You must tell me."

"When I came back after first seeing the police." Brita hoped that she'd done the right thing by telling him about it. It felt good to get it off her chest. She noticed that Ron's expression suddenly changed from easygoing to concerned. "I must get back to work. Thanks for the answers." She started to back away.

"Wait." Ron caught her arm. "Let's have dinner later. What time works best for you? I can get someone to cover for me, most anytime." Ron softened his voice. "How about eight? We'll sit in the back where it's quieter, and we can talk about all of this in private."

"It's almost that now. Twenty minutes in the dining car." Brita walked briskly away.

*****

The killer sat back and watched the interaction between Ron and Brita, listening carefully. As yet, the rumors about the murder seemed to conclude it was a normal gangster killing. When he'd searched inside of Brita's room for further information and left the knife with a picture of Charlot Fortier, he'd seen that she was returning and he'd had to hurry. Rushing never did any good, and he cursed himself for accidentally leaving the door ajar.

The message that he'd sent to his informant in Burlington was short and brisk, informing him of the delay. He'd also sent one to an informant who would pass the word on to his commander about the assassination. The Fuhrer would be pleased once he learned who had been executed.

*****

When Brita walked away, Ron turned his thoughts to the opened room door. He was certain that she'd locked it. He was going to have to keep his eyes and ears open and try to investigate on his own without raising any suspicions.

Ron had forgotten that he had a customer by the bar until he heard the man belch.

"Sorry. How about another beer? Name's George, what's yours?" He slid the empty bottle across the countertop to Ron. He straightened his wide lapels from his pin-striped suit and blue silk necktie.

"Name's Ron." Ron handed the bottle over and took the money. He noticed Mr. Swensen coming over to him.

"When do you think this silver bullet will get rolling? I'm getting anxious, ol' chap," Swensen said. "How about a Schell's?"

"One beer coming right up." Ron opened the bottle and set it before him.

"Thanks." Swensen handed over the cash. He drank his beer and walked away.

Ron turned his attention back to the other customers in the full room. He noticed that Jacques and Carlo were still playing dice, only it looked as though Swensen might join them. *Three high-rolling sots*, Ron thought.

*****

When Brita walked away, she tried to put Ron out of her thoughts, but found it difficult. She took a moment to stop and look out of one of the many windows along the corridor, which ran the length of the car. Brita started hiking toward the passenger car. A train whooshed alongside of the Zephyr when they passed through an intersection, where lights flashed and bells clanged.

Brita walked down the aisle and fetched a newspaper for a gentleman, then showed a woman how to switch on the overhead light. Another woman needed simple directions as to how to lean the seat back. After she'd finished walking through the car, Brita found that she was completely exhausted.

The train's length was endless. She glanced at her watch. At last was time to meet Ron.

Brita went directly to her room. She stepped inside and reached for her bag, quickly reapplying her makeup. When that was done, she straightened her hose and skirt, then brushed out her wavy hair. When her uniform hat was in place, she gave herself a quick look. She put the list of names inside her suitcase before stepping back out the door.

A door creaked open as Brita locked hers. It felt like someone was watching her, and she turned to look. When she didn't see anyone, Brita walked away.

"Oh! Father O'Malley!" she said, almost walking into him. "Sorry, I wasn't looking."

"No problem. I was busy thinking about the good food and my next sermon." He gave her a quick smile before continuing.

The list of names went through Brita's mind, and she wished that she could remember if his was one of them. Several were recognizable, but most weren't, and it was troublesome. Any one of the men could've been the killer. Brita realized that she was going to have to put her deduction skills into practice, since it seemed that the agents weren't going to be able to figure it out.

"The dinner was really good," Rose said when they met up in the corridor. "I'm sure that you'll enjoy it."

"Thanks. I'm sure that I will," Brita said. She could feel her stomach grumbling.

With each step closer to the dining car, her stomach growled louder. She hadn't realized that she was so hungry. By the time she'd walked into the lounge area, she was certain that she could eat a buffalo… but a chicken dinner would do.

Ron wasn't at work, and she continued hiking to the dining car. Brita looked into the doorway. The man who reminded her of Al Capone or John Dillinger—because of his loose fitting, pin-striped suit and blue silk tie—was seated alone. Ron was seated in the back corner. He glanced her way and smiled. She headed straight toward him.

"I took the liberty and ordered us each a chicken dinner." He noticed that she'd just put on fresh lipstick, which delighted him. "Do you mind?"

"Not at all," she said, sliding into her seat. "You must've read my mind." Brita noticed that he'd smoothed his collar down over the tie, rearranging it from the last time she'd seen him. A twinkle sparkled in her eye, and she smiled at him.

Chapter Six

The killer squinted as he climbed the stairs into the observation deck. He found a secluded chair off to the side and sat.

The train began rocking and rolling, and he was delighted to finally leave the depot and the investigation behind him.

As the train wound around past the stockyards, he saw the limestone arch with the large head of a cow in the top center. It made him think of his true mission: poisoning the nation's beef supply in Omaha. During the OSS investigation, it had been quite easy for him to go unnoticed as he studied the elevators and how the grain was surged from one bin to the next. He'd even filched some spilled grain and placed it in an empty tobacco tin before returning to the train.

Gradually the Zephyr began to pick up energy, and he watched the landscape change as the train rolled out of town. It seemed so long ago that he'd lived in St. Paul, Minnesota, yet it had only been a mere twenty years. His thoughts went to his father. Prohibition had changed his life because of the feds always hunting him down and throwing him in jail. Herr Hitler's National Socialist German Worker's Party policy had enabled his father to have immediate employment, so they moved back home to Germany. Herr Hitler took care of families through immediate factory jobs. His father never had liked Americans and their boastfulness about how great they thought they were—Germans were smarter and stronger.

Voices began to fill the room. The observation deck was filling up, and he knew that his luck of being alone had ended. He turned on the overhead light, spread open the Chicago Tribune and began to read.

Someone bumped into his knees. He glanced over the edge

of the newspaper at the offending newcomer. "Yes?" he growled.

"Oh… excuse me. My name is Rose." She sat down, noticed the chilling look in his eye, and shivered. Nervously, she straightened her skirt and felt her French roll, making sure that all the pins were in place.

"That's quite all right," he replied. She peered at him as if she were going to say something, and he quickly went back to looking at the paper. Panic started to creep into his soul.

He recognized her.

"Aren't you…" she said slowly, tapping her fingers on his knee. "Hmm… let me think now. Aren't you… Iggy? Yes! That's it. You're Iggy from down by Swede Hollow in St. Paul, aren't you?" She grinned. "We were playmates. You liked to climb trees. You didn't like closed spaces. You never liked playing in our backyard treehouse. We always had to be in wide-open spaces."

"No ma'am, you've got me mixed up with someone else," he murmured. As he stared at the paper, he felt fear rising to the surface. He sucked in a few long breaths to try and stay calm.

"You lived in that little yellow house," she said sweetly. Pulling the edge of the paper down, she saw his face clearly. "I'm positive it's you. I can tell by the arch over your eye." Rose gave him a smile, holding down the newspaper. "And that peculiar mole on your ear. I always thought it was dirt and would wash away."

"Lady, you've got me mixed up with someone else," he grouched. "Now if you'll excuse me." He briskly folded the newspaper, and was about to stand up when she clung to his arm.

"I don't think so," Rose said, overly sweet. Her fingers clung onto his suit coat like pincers. "Didn't you use to play kickball all the time, but used your left foot even though you're right handed? Still play baseball?"

"Excuse me." He slid his right hand inside his pocket and

briskly walked away. He glanced at the other passengers in the observation deck and was relieved that none of them seemed to have been paying any attention. A ripple of fear raced up and down his spine as he descended the steps. Iggy died a long time ago, and needed to remain buried.

Chapter Seven

The dining room smelled of roast chicken and the strong scent of sage stuffing. Brita smiled at the colorful flowers put in vases, which sat upon each tabletop.

"I'd like to order wine, but we aren't allowed, unless you think Burlington wouldn't notice?" Ron noticed that she was the prettiest when she smiled.

"It's probably not a good idea," Brita said. She giggled, and decided that the meal was going to be fun. As she removed the napkin ring, Brita thought the white linen tablecloth was beautiful against the silverware. "Chicago's the Windy City… and it never stops blowing here, does it?"

"The city lives up to its reputation," Ron replied. He swallowed hard because of the lump in his throat. "I think that I should learn more about you, since we seem to be crossing each other's path all the time."

They both looked up as Harold walked over with two glasses of wine and set them down.

"I won't tell," Harold said with a wink.

"Thanks," they said in unison. They raised their glasses as Harold walked away.

"What are we toasting?" Brita asked.

"Making it through the last twenty-four hours," Ron said. "We both deserve this glass, Brita." He gave her a bright smile before taking a sip.

"I agree. To us." She took a sip, then set the glass down. "So tell me, Ron, why was I spared? Why wasn't I murdered, too? I don't understand it for one minute." She shook her head and leaned forward, staring into his eyes. "I'm scared."

"Me too. I'm scared for you. Here's what I think happened."

He took a drink before continuing. "I think that they didn't know that anyone was following them. When you fell and snapped the branch and twigs, the killer must have wondered if he'd been spotted. He killed Mindel, then assaulted you, knocking you out. He must've figured that you didn't see anything." Ron watched as she swirled the wine in her glass before taking another drink. He noted how petite she was. Brita was all beauty… Ron understood why the general made it clear to "keep his fucking hands" off her.

"You could be right about that," she conceded. She took another sip. "But that doesn't mean that I'm not still in danger. I sure as heck would like to know who killed Mindel. I feel responsible. If only I hadn't tripped and made so much noise, then maybe he could've been saved." Tears suddenly welled in her eyes, and she wiped them dry. "Sorry."

"No problem," Ron said. He finished his wine. "Drink up, you'll feel better. It wasn't your fault. Let's call it fate's hand… the gun could've easily been turned on you as well if you'd tried to intervene." He stared into her eyes. He let out a long sigh of relief when he saw Harold carrying the plates. "I think our meal is coming. Now we can think about food instead of what could've happened." *Or each other,* he'd wanted to say.

"Enjoy your dinner," Harold said. He set down the full plates, plus a small dinner roll and butter on the side for each of them. "Would you care for coffee?"

"I'd love it," Brita answered. The smell of the roast chicken made her mouth water, and she licked her lips. Golden gravy spilled over the lip of the snow-white mashed potatoes and onto the sides of the plate. She scooped up a bite and tasted it. The gravy was yummier than her grandma's, and she beamed after swallowing it. "This is heavenly." She took another bite.

"This is delicious," Ron echoed at almost the same time.

As they ate, Ron glanced around the room. He hadn't had a chance to ask for a passenger list, but it was number one on his agenda. He scanned the other diners, but no one seemed suspicious. The man dressed in a suit and tie and sitting alone was probably a beef buyer and heading for Omaha—or Burlington, Iowa—and buying corn for market. Ron turned his attention back to Brita.

"Tell me about the passengers. Do you know any of them, or recognize them from the Twin Cities Z?" He took a drink of his wine before cutting into his chicken breast. "Boy, this is moist."

"I haven't had a chance to compare the rosters yet, but I remember him," she responded, nodding towards the suited man seated behind them. She took a drink of coffee, then took a bite of the chicken. "It sure is juicy," she replied after she'd finished swallowing her bite of food. "Let's see—I know that a middle-aged woman named Rose was on the other train. Oh, and I just remembered that priest, Father O'Malley. She looked out the window for a moment in thought before continuing, "Um…Carlo and Jacques, and two couples in our sleeping coach. I believe their names are Bakko and Magnusson." She took another bite and shrugged.

"That's all that you remember?" Ron asked. When she nodded, he said, "It's a good start." He tried to fit an image together with the name. Ron was thankful for her help, because now he had a suspect list. However it didn't seem like any of the passengers she'd mentioned were capable of cold-blooded murder.

Brita was relieved that he didn't ask her any more questions. As they sat in comfortable silence, she cleaned her plate and set it aside. Reaching for her coffee, she took a moment to study him… and found him to be the most handsome man that she'd ever set her eyes on.

"What are you thinking?" Ron asked. He dropped his napkin on the plate.

"Work."

"I'll take your plates," Harold said, coming by and interrupting.

"Why don't I walk you through the lounge so that the three highrollers won't whistle in case they've returned?" Ron inquired, and grinned when she giggled.

"I think I will take you up on your offer, but don't you have to work?"

"Don't worry, I'll go back to the lounge." Ron pushed back his chair.

They walked out of the dining car. They hurried into the lounge because of the sudden cold rush of air.

One card table was lined with players, and smoke hovered above them. The booth where the three high rollers had been was vacant.

"People must be getting ready for bed," Ron said. They passed through the almost-empty room.

"Or else they're just tired of sitting and figure that time will go faster if they move around."

"You could be right."

He led her through the empty corridor and into the following vestibule.

"I have work to do," she said softly.

"I know." Ron gazed into her eyes and leaned over until their lips touched.

His kiss took Brita's breath away.

"Good night." Ron stared into her warm eyes, then kissed her.

"You too," she stammered, staring at him. The kiss was so light, but left her breathless. "I must get busy. I have to go up to check on the passengers before going to bed." She had to force herself to leave.

*****

As Ron walked away, the general's warning circling around in his head. With Brita, he felt as if he reached another galaxy, with Margot… he had only touched the sun.

Ron went back to the lounge and wiped down the counters and booths. As he cleaned, he let his thoughts go to Brita and the murder.

The other person in the photo besides Poloski's kid's teacher was also a scientist, and teaching at the University of Chicago… which was why he assumed that Mindel was one as well. His knowledge was dead-ended after that. Something nagged at him, and it had to do with the knot on Mindel's necktie. He'd slipped on so many ties in his life that it was second nature to tie them. However, this particular knot was different. It wasn't a Windsor. He'd realized that there'd been an extra step added to the knot. Ron wondered if there was a connection involving a tie with another murder. He'd feel much better once he learned the truth about it.

He looked up to see Swensen enter.

"Beer?"

"No. Make it a shot of whiskey for a change."

"Where's the other two? Did you beat them out of their money?" Ron set it up for him.

"Nope. They're filling some dames with bullshit. Thanks." Swensen raised the glass to his lips and drank it down. "Ahh…" he said, setting it back onto the counter. He went to sit in the dark window seat.

*****

Brita walked from one coach to the next, checking on passengers. In one of the cars, she noticed the two sailors sitting and staring out at the black sky.

"If it isn't my two knights in shining armor." She walked up to them. "Are you enjoying the view?"

"You bet," John said. "How's it going? Been in a bind, lately?" He gave her a wink and a grin.

"Hey! You hear anything at all about any of that?" Ax asked. He sat straighter and motioned to a chair. "Have a seat and tell us what happened. We were both kinda wonderin'." He glanced around to make sure that no one was paying them any attention.

"Sure. For just a bit." She sat across from them. "Actually, you fellas know just as much as I do." She reached out and touched John's arm. "That's the God's honest truth."

"Serious?" John said. "I don't believe it. Who do you think did it?"

"We're just lucky to have seen you," Ax said with a big grin.

"Boy, that's for sure. It was so dark, and I was so tired." Brita gave them a thankful smile.

"Do you think the killer is on the train?" John asked. He looked closely at her.

"Nope. If he was, the train wouldn't be moving." Brita looked hard into each of their eyes. "Now I must get busy and keep moving."

"We'll keep a close eye on our 'damsel in distress', won't we, Ax?" John said. He had a twinkle in his eye.

"You bet."

"I'll remember that," Brita responded lightheartedly. "Thanks again."

When Brita walked away, the nagging feeling returned of something that wasn't quite right. She stopped for a moment, watching the shadows of the city disappear into the night. It felt as if the train was moving faster and faster because the streetlights blurred into one big glimmer. It took but a short moment for the train to pass over the Fox River trestle. The Fox River ran into the Illinois River, which eventually met the Mississippi River.

Someone passed beside her, jolting her back to the present. She decided to head for the observation deck. As she approached the stairs, several people were climbing down, forcing her to step aside. When she reached the top of the stairs and had a chance to look out onto the vast prairie lands, it seemed odd to see such total darkness except for the light from the train. In the distance, she noticed a light shutting off in a window, which was the only life that she saw.

Toward the front of the panoramic windows, Brita saw the lady who liked knitting click on a Crackerjack cricket and talk at the same time. A piece of work lay on her lap like a blanket, and she sat tapping a needle against a smoking pipe. Her thick brows arched as if in a puzzle, and her big brown eyes kept the quizzical look of a permanent question mark. The purple hat on her head, along with the silver-gray hair sticking out from under the round base, reminded Brita of a pincushion. Brita smiled, and walked over to older woman.

"Hello, I'm Brita. What in the world are you doing?" When Brita looked deeper in her eyes, she saw exactly what she'd suspected she'd see… the sharpness and wisdom of age, with a touch of eccentricity.

"I'm Ella, and it's grand to sit back and just look out, even if it is dark outside." She nodded to the empty chair opposite her. "Have a seat and I'll tell you." She placed a small piece of a knitted section against the pipe and tapped it. "Not right yet," she mused, shaking her head. Afterwards, she picked up the knitting and began threading the yarn through her fingers like an extra pair of hands.

"Not right yet? What do you mean, Ella?" Brita did as she was told and sat. The smug smile on Ella's lips and the arch of her brow made Brita wonder if she was a fruitcake. "I'm all ears."

"You've heard me on the radio." Ella leaned closer to Brita as she clicked the needles louder. "Hear that sound? That was used in the *Amos 'n' Andy* show just last week!" She grinned. "Ever heard footsteps or sirens, or a woman scream?" When Brita nodded, she said, "It was probably me." She chuckled.

"You're kidding?!" Brita's mouth gaped open from shock, and she quickly covered it. "I don't believe it." She thought about all the sound effects on the stations. "How did you do that sound when Pepsodent sponsored the bright smile? That whoosh sound?"

"I blew into a bag," Ella said. Ella's coal black eyes made her eyebrows look like quotation marks. She laughed at Brita's expression.

"I don't know what to say," Brita said, gigging uncontrollably. "You're the shoes and choo-choo train?" Tears streamed down her cheeks from laughter, and she reached for a handkerchief to wipe her nose and eyes. "What sound were you trying to perfect just now?"

"I'm not altogether sure yet, but I'll let you know when I have it figured out." Ella leaned in ever closer to Brita and whispered, "It is kinda funny, ain't it?"

"Yes. You're a star." Brita gave her a big smile. "I should get back to work, now that I know you're not a nut." She chuckled. "Maybe I should ask for your autograph?"

"Don't be silly. Stop by sometime, and I'll show you my bag of tricks." Ella patted Brita's knee like an aunt would. "You'd be surprised at all the junk I carry around with me." She grinned and looked up toward the back. "Here comes the biggest gossip mill of all time. Honey, we'll keep in touch." She nodded toward Gladys, who had just entered.

"I must get busy." Brita wiped her eyes. "Thanks." Brita walked over to Gladys.

"I'm calling it a day," Gladys said, yawning. "You can too. Don't think about the murder or anything. Just push it completely out of your mind, and then you'll sleep like a baby. Remember, just push it right out..." She motioned with her hand. "Get it?" She snapped her fingers.

"You betcha," Brita said, zooming right past her. *Thanks for reminding me so that I'll think about it all night long, Brita thought ruefully.*

Brita stopped a moment to listen to the announcement.

Folks! I hope that I'm not interrupting your sleep, but take a minute to look out to the Northwest, and you just might be able to see Bishop Hill. It's the site where the first settlers arrived on the Illinois prairie in 1846. It was founded by a group of Swedish religious dissidents. The village has existed for many years. Over and out!

When Stan finished, Brita continued toward the sleeping car, and her room. As she entered the next passenger car, she met Rose by the women's restroom.

Rose stopped Brita. "I have a favor to ask of you, if you don't mind?"

"What is it?" Brita asked.

"I get motion sickness sometimes. I wonder if you wouldn't check on me in the morning? Just knock and take a quick look-see to make sure that I'm fine. I don't need breakfast, because it makes me nauseated when I'm on a train. Will you do that?" She gave Brita's hand a quick squeeze.

"Sure. Not a problem."

"You're a dear." Rose entered the restroom.

Brita thought of Ron as she finally entered her room. She wondered if he was married, but she didn't think so. He was so self-assured and full of confidence. He'd made her feel safe… still did, if she was honest with herself.

Brita flicked on her light before plunking down on the bed. His kiss had given her goose pimples. While replaying every word that had been said between them, she noticed a shadow of someone's shoes against the strip of light underneath the door. She shut off the light, and held her breath. As she listened to the retreating footsteps, her heart pounded. She wondered if her mind was playing tricks on her.

Brita opened the door slowly and peered out, seeing nothing. She shut the door and locked it while her heart raced with fear.

Brita reached for her suitcase and opened it up. She threw her nightclothes on top of the bed.

After sliding the uniform off and slipping into her nightgown, Brita crawled into bed. Her mind raced. Last night's trek through the rail yard replayed, and she repeated every footstep and every inch that she'd walked. She pictured the gunman and Mindel, then saw him dead. Tears flooded her eyes. The tree that she'd hid behind came to mind, as well as the memory of tripping over the root and breaking the branch was the final thing that she saw or remembered. She wished that she could have heard what was said between the two men. With all of her might, Brita tried to picture the gunman. All that came to mind was that he was taller than Mindel and walked with a slouch.

She tried shutting her eyes and focusing on pleasanter happenings, such as the trip ahead of her. After tossing and turning for forty minutes, she finally gave up and reached for the light switch.

Once she'd turned it on, Brita reached for *Gone with the Wind.* She found her missing knife with what appeared to be a photograph wrapped around it in the book's secret compartment. With shaky fingers, she picked it up and cautiously unfolded the picture.

The knife's point was inserted into the photograph through Charlot Fortier's chest.

Brita's eyes opened wide. She dropped the picture and reached for a handkerchief as tears filled her eyes. Clutching the handkerchief tight within her fist, she held it over her mouth as the realization hit her like a bolt. Her good friend had been murdered.

She was next on the list. The sudden shock shrouded her mind, and she fainted onto the bed.

*****

The killer slipped into the compartment after deftly picking the lock. The diversion of an elderly passenger requiring assistance from the porter had allowed him to enter the car without anyone noticing.

After he undid his tie, he quickly took a heavy streetcar token from his pants and slipped it into a tie pocket at the end. Swinging it back and forth, he tested its weight. Wrapping it about his hand, he flicked the heavier end out and was satisfied with his substitute garrote.

"Sorry, Rose. You know too much," he said softly. "I'll be as painless as possible."

She really didn't deserve to die, he thought with each flick of the wrist.

The twist of a key alerted him, and he moved behind the door. As soon as Rose stepped inside, he quickly closed the door behind her as he flicked the heavier end around her neck. Grabbing it with his other hand, he swiftly crossed his wrists and brought his knee into her back. With a sharp and practiced jerk, he broke her neck.

Before the door had banged shut, he'd neatly placed her on the bed. With his thumb and forefinger, he loosened her jaw and slipped a silver dollar on her tongue.

"To pay the ferryman's price," he whispered.

Chapter Eight

Brita bolted upright during the night from a bad dream. She saw the figure of the murderer chasing her into a black hole where skeletons lay in mounds, and as she passed them, they sat up and began following her one by one. Mindel's image chased after her, overpowering the figure as he struggled to catch her with opened, knife-like fingers.

Sweat beaded her brow and perspiration moistened her armpits as she realized that the picture and knife lay beside her. She swung her legs over the side of the bed and stood up. The nightgown spilled over her slim frame like a thin veil. She stared out the window for a few minutes, trying to slow her racing heart.

The silver rays of the moon spread like a blanket across the fields and pastures, as if lulling them to sleep while the train passed them by.

Brita opened the knife and wiped it clean, letting out a long breath when it revealed a lack of blood on the linen. Somehow it made her feel better knowing that her knife wasn't used in the murder. After placing the derringer under her pillow, she closed the knife and hid it under the mattress. She put the picture in her purse.

Brita knew that she wouldn't be able to get back to sleep. She crawled between the sheets again and glanced at the doorway where a thread of corridor lights shone under the threshold. The comfort of familiar voices echoing through the walls warmed her heart. Brita reached up and turned on the radio that she'd borrowed from Dwight before drawing the covers up under her chin. In the relative stillness, she listened to the blues station that was broadcast from Chicago, the only other sound the clacking of the rails. It took her mind off her troubles. Her thoughts went to her former fiancé, Winston, and how she'd vowed after they'd split to never fall in love again. Winston had run off with a former girlfriend and married her right after enlisting. That was two years before. Since then, her heart hadn't completely mended.

Brita made up her mind that it didn't matter how good Ron's kisses tasted, she would not let him or any other man win her heart. She rolled over and fell into a fitful sleep.

*****

The radio station was off the air, and the background static woke her. She reached up and shut it off. A passing train rumbled right outside her window, jiggling the Zephyr. When it passed, a riverboat chugged and blew its horn, and she knew that they were almost to Burlington. Brita yawned and tried to fall back asleep but couldn't, as fear kept intruding. Giving up, she slid into her robe and decided to step out of her compartment for fresh air.

Dwight was carrying an extra blanket into Father O'Malley's compartment.

"Do you need any help?" She walked softly toward him.

"No. It's four a.m., go back to sleep." Dwight shook his head at her.

"The passing train woke me up. I just needed to stretch." Brita yawned, as if in emphasis.

"Good night," Dwight said, sounding slightly annoyed.

Grumbling to herself, Brita returned to her compartment and crawled back under the sheets. She tossed fitfully until sleep finally claimed her.

Day three

Finger slits of sunlight streamed through the window blinds and settled on her eyelids. Brita groaned and rolled over, tugging the blanket over her head. As she thought about getting up, there was a knock upon her door.

"Six o'clock, Brita. Time to get up," Dwight said as he rapped softly on the door.

"Okay." Brita sighed and punched the pillow.

A door closed, and a passenger coughed and spat, then coughed again. He then cleared his gruff voice before blowing his nose.

"Shoot!" Brita grouched. "Can't he cough any quieter?"

Brita's itchy eyes burned. She forced her legs over the side of the bed. Her watch read ten minutes after six. She didn't have much time to dawdle, since her duties began when she left her room. Plus she had to check in on Rose.

As she let the water run for a quick wash-up, she stared at the mirrored reflection of her dry, bloodshot eyes. She rinsed her face, brushed her teeth, and combed her hair.

The blue uniform slid nicely over her hips, and a hint of a cleavage showed through the suit coat. She rolled the silk stockings up over her knees and hitched them onto the garter belt. Beside the garter belt, she wore a small pocket where she placed the knife. She left the derringer under the pillow. She slipped her feet into flat-sole shoes that felt like slippers, and finally felt ready to get started with her day.

When Brita stepped out into the corridor, she looked down the aisle toward Ron's room and wondered how well he had slept. She turned and started for Rose's compartment at the other end of the car. As she came closer the vestibule door opened, surprising her.

"I knew there'd be fresh ones," Ella said. She jiggled a white bag, beaming from ear to ear.

"What have we here?" Brita grinned. "You must've bought doughnuts." She put her hands on her hips, and chuckled. "I can smell them, and they're making my stomach growl."

"You bet, you're right on the button," Ella laughed. "Took this train once before, and I almost melted when I ate these Long Johns. I just had to have another one or three." Her eyes twinkled. "Got time to join me?" She headed for her door.

"Not right now, but hopefully I will in a short while. Will

you save me one?" Brita asked, and hoped that she would.

"If you hurry." Ella opened her room and went inside.

"Hmm, might have to go myself," Brita mused. A chocolate covered doughnut did sound awfully good, along with the Long Johns.

Brita kept walking until she arrived at Rose's door, then knocked.

"Rose. Time to wake up. Rose?" Brita knocked again, and looked at her watch. It was 6:30. "Rose? Say something so that I know you're still in there. I'll go and get you coffee or tea, if you'd like."

Something didn't seem right. Brita looked over and saw Dwight walking toward her.

"Have you seen Rose this morning?"

"Hmm, let me see," Dwight said, rubbing his chin. "No. I think she stayed in her room all night. She might have gotten up once. Yes… I did see her once." He gave her a puzzled look. "Why?"

"She should've answered," Brita said with concern. "This doesn't seem right. I hope she didn't get too nauseated… maybe she's a very sound sleeper." Brita wondered if that was the case, but remembered how insistent Rose was about Brita checking up on her.

"Maybe she snuck out for doughnuts, too," Dwight said with a wink.

"No. She doesn't eat breakfast on a train," Brita explained to Dwight. "Rose! Time to wake up." She pounded on the door and tried to open it. Turning to Dwight, she asked, "Do you have a key? I think we'd better check inside. She gave me strict orders to check on her in the morning. If you haven't seen her, then maybe she's sick. She should've answered." Brita frowned, hoping that Rose wouldn't be mad if she was sleeping.

"Move aside," Dwight said. He took out his large key ring, then slipped the numbered key into the hole and turned the knob, opening the door. "Rose?"

Rose lay on top of the made bed, face up, still wearing the clothes from the day before. Her head was turned at an odd angle, and her right arm dangled over the side of the bed.

"Rose? Are you still sleeping?" Brita tentatively walked to her and touched her shoulder. "Rose. Wake up. Rose?" With trembling fingers Brita tried to shake her awake, but her gut told her that Rose was permanently sleeping. "I don't believe this." Brita picked up Rose's wrist and felt for a pulse, then did the same on her neck. Staring at Dwight, she whispered, "I think Rose is dead." She began trembling. "She's dead!" she cried.

"Dead?" Dwight looked at Brita's ashen face, then opened his arms as she collapsed into them. He settled her into the corner on the floor. "Wake up. Brita! Brita!" He slightly shook her. "Damn. Brita! Wake up!"

*****

Ron was in the middle of carrying a passenger's luggage back to the compartment when he heard the commotion. After he'd finished returning the suitcase, he quickly rushed to Rose's door and saw Dwight fanning Brita.

"What happened?" Then he saw Rose and the stillness of her body, and instinct took over. "Go and get the conductor, then immediately come back here. Don't speak to anyone." His stare and authoritative voice demanded Dwight's attention. Ron's heart flip-flopped when he looked at Brita's pale face.

"Yes, of course." Dwight helped Brita sit and whispered, "I'll be right back." Brita mouthed, "Okay."

"I'll lock the door so that no one accidentally enters. This has to be kept secret." Dwight left, locking the door behind him.

Ron checked Rose's body and confirmed his fears. Rose was most definitely dead. The odd angle of her head made him almost certain it was not an accident. He turned back to Brita.

"Brita?" Crouching down beside her, Ron softly stroked her cheek and smoothed the hair from her face. As she slowly opened her eyes, he thought about how beautiful they were.

"Brita? Tell me what happened." He raised her chin up and briefly touched her lips with his thumb.

"I need a drink of water," Brita whispered. Tentatively, she gave him a smile.

"Sure." Ron stood up and poured a small glass for her. "Here." He handed it over. "Are you better?" When she nodded, he took the empty glass and set it down on the counter. "Good. Now can you tell me what happened?" Taking her hands in his, he whispered, "I'm ready when you are."

"I think I'll stay down here for a few more minutes, if that's okay?" She stared into his eyes, and the kindness in them warmed her heart. "I'm suddenly cold."

"Here, put my coat around your shoulders." She leaned forward, and he draped it over her. "Now can you tell me exactly what happened, how you found the body?"

"I walked in here, and this is what I saw. I was worried because Rose had asked me to check on her in the morning, but she didn't answer my knock. Dwight opened the door. I checked her pulse, and then I must have fainted."

"Take your time, but I want you to look around the room and see if it appears as if anything is amiss." Ron let go of her hands. "I'm going to take a look in her purse and suitcase." He handed her a handkerchief before standing.

"Thanks." Her eyes filled with tears. She blew her nose.

"We don't have much time." Ron glanced at her before opening the purse. In her wallet, he found a library card from St. Paul, a few coins, plus a couple of dollars.

"Help me up," Brita said. She reached for his hand. His hand felt so strong and warm, and her heart skipped. "I should've stayed in the military; it would've been a lot safer," she thought out loud.

"I doubt it. There's a war going on, remember?" Ron held her close for a minute, before pulling away.

"I feel so bad. Rose should be alive." Brita took a closer look at Rose. "She sure wore a lot of makeup."

"I agree," he said, continuing to search the purse.

"I feel sick," Brita said. She clutched her stomach. "This is giving me the creeps. Dead people make me feel funny."

"Don't vomit yet…" He winked. "Wait until Dwight comes."

"I won't vomit." She frowned. "Look." She pointed to the smeared makeup on Rose's neck. "She had a birthmark that she was trying to cover up. See?"

"Oh yes." Ron stared at the spot. "Looks like something rubbed some of her makeup of. I wonder…" There was a knock on the door. "They're back."

"Sorry, we were busy talking," Ron said, opening the door. "She's just as she was found."

Stan barged into the room as Dwight quickly closed the door behind him. Gone was the ever-present smile and grandfatherly demeanor. In one swift stride, he was standing over the body. "We need a doctor immediately. She's awfully cold, and I don't feel a pulse. I'll alert the engineer when we stop the train, and he can contact the stationmaster after the doctor's examination."

"I wonder how she died," Dwight said, rubbing his chin. He walked over to the body. "Interesting… very interesting." He studied it. "Probably went to sleep and never woke up. A heart attack."

"Dwight?" Stan took charge of the situation.

"Ahh… yes?" Dwight looked at Stan.

"There's a doctor in coach number ten. I believe his name is Feinstein. Get him immediately. Don't speak to anyone. Just tell him that someone needs his services and say no more. Understood?"

"Yes. Understood." Dwight left, locking the door behind him.

Stan turned his attention back to Ron and Brita.

"Tell me how it happened that you two ended up in here with yet another death on your hands?" He glanced at Brita, who was a ball of tears.

"Poor Rose," Brita whispered. She blew her nose.

"What's that?" Ron's eye caught a glimmer of something that had fallen into the corner by the door. He went over and picked it up. "It's a Seattle streetcar token. Probably just dropped from her pocket."

Brita began to take mental notes of everything in the room. The book Rose had been reading was sitting out, as well as an open newspaper and her brush and comb. Nothing seemed to be touched or out of place.

"Let's start from the top." Stan removed his black cap. "Now, one at a time, tell me exactly what happened and how." Stan slipped his cap back on. The train seemed to rock a little, and he said, "We're waiting for clearance to approach the station. Go ahead."

"Last night Rose had asked me to check on her this morning, which I did. There wasn't an answer so I had Dwight open the door, and this is how we found her." Brita looked over to Ron who nodded his approval.

"I heard noise and came running only to find Brita on the floor and Dwight bending over her and Rose still on the bed. I asked Dwight to go find you." Ron gave him a tentative smile. "I hope it was a heart attack."

"Me, too," Stan replied. "Not a word about this to anyone, you two... especially not a passenger. We don't need to get them panicked. After Chicago, it wouldn't take much. Oh... better not tell Gladys, or it will be rumor city in ten minutes."

"I wish that Dwight would hurry with the doctor," Stan remarked, studying the body. "Who'da thought? She's young." He scratched his whiskers.

"It almost seems like Rose was trying to tell us something." Brita looked at the newspaper. "I wonder why she had the paper open to this page? Do you think there's any significance to it?"

"What's that? I'm sorry, I was thinking...." Stan looked over to her. "Oh yes, the newspaper? I have no idea." He raised his brow.

"Interesting." Ron ran his fingers through his hair as sweat beads popped out on his brow. Rose knew something, but what, he wondered? What a puzzle, he mused. "Would you mind if we opened her suitcase and looked through it?

"Leave it to the authorities. It's time for you two to go back to your compartments. Stay there until you've been given further instructions." Stan took out his watch and glanced at the time. "I wish the doctor and Dwight would hurry up and come. It won't be long until the passengers will be lining up and hollering for their baggage." Stan ran his hand through his hair and then looked over at Rose. "I'm covering her up so no one can see her." He reached for the overhead blanket.

"You'll know where to find us," Ron said, opening the door. He ushered Brita out first.

The aisle was filling with spectators— with Gladys at the forefront—just as the train began to glide into the station.

*****

The killer enjoyed watching the scene unfold in front of him.

He was certain that Rose remembered that his father worked in the petroleum factories, and that Herr Hitler was one of his idols, since their mothers had corresponded until the United States entered the war.

That makeshift garrote had been quite efficient, he thought, rubbing his chin before allowing himself a smile.

*****

Dwight opened the door and let the doctor step inside first.

"Right here," Stan said. He uncovered the body when the door closed. "This is as she was found."

"Yes. Nothing is disturbed. Brita and I walked in and found her just like this," Dwight answered.

"Good. Now let's let him do his job," Stan said. He moved beside Dwight.

"Let's see now...." Doctor Feinstein placed his hands alongside Rose's neck and then opened her eyelids. "Her eyes are bulging, and her neck is broken." Pulling her jaw open, he found a coin on top of her tongue. "Interesting, indeed. Call the authorities and the coroner. They'll want a complete examination done immediately."

"That's what I didn't want to hear," Stan said, and sighed. "We'll lock up the room for now. Dwight, you're to stay outside and make sure that no one enters. Understood?"

"Yes." Dwight said.

"Doctor, keep us informed as to where you are in case you're needed again," Stan ordered.

"I'll be where I was found." Doctor Feinstein looked at Dwight, and they nodded to each other.

"You may both go. Matter of fact, I'm going to see the engineer straight away. We'll leave together." Stan looked at Dwight. "Give me the key so that I can get back in here." He took it from Dwight and put it in his pocket. "Let's go."

When the door opened, there was a flurry of voices until it was shut again.

"Bet we won't leave for Omaha for a long time," Dr. Feinstein said.

"Bet you're right," Stan replied, matter-of-factly.

Stan and the doctor slipped around the crowd of people, ignoring everyone. Dwight stood in front of the door like a sentry, never saying a word.

*****

Ron paced the room until he thought he'd wear out the floor. He massaged his chin and stopped in front of the window and stared at the Mississippi River.

Something wasn't right about the whole scenario, but he couldn't figure out what it was. Ron reached into his wallet and removed his badge and looked at it. He clutched it in the palm of his hand and closed his eyes, searching his mind for every little detail about Mindel's murder.

Mindel had been a scientist, but Rose certainly wasn't. There weren't any signs of a struggle, so that meant that the killer had been hiding. The two deaths were too close to Brita, which meant that he must be alert and protective. Unless he could figure out a common thread between Mindel, Rose, and the missing Dr. Fortier, he'd have no reason behind his nagging suspicions.

Sinking into his bed, Ron shut his eyes and let his mind fill with random thoughts as he waited for Stan.

*****

When Ron's arm was draped over her shoulder, Brita had felt better… all warm and safe. She'd hated to say goodbye to him, and hated herself for wanting him to kiss her again. She had to admit Ron sure made her feel good, but Brita was certain that most of his attention was due to the previous murder, and now Rose's death. She remembered the knife and picture and shivered, hoping that the killer would be caught.

Brita stared out the side window and watched as people came and went from the train. She recalled the bag of doughnuts and Ella's kind offer, and wondered if she dared go to visit her. The knock on her door made her jump, and she looked toward it.

"Come in," she called. Brita swung her legs around to the floor. She opened the door a crack to peek out and saw Ella.

"Thought you'd like your doughnut." Ella stood holding the little white bag. "I went for more, and had just returned when I saw that the corridor was all abuzz like a beehive. When I asked, I heard all sorts of stories, so I thought that I'd take my chances and pound on your door. And here you are. Now, can you tell me about it?" Ella smiled at her and shook the bag.

"Sorry, but I'm not supposed to. Excuse my poor manners, but I was just thinking about your offer," Brita said. She wiped her moist eyes and blew her nose. She stepped aside to let Ella enter, and quickly shut the door. "Such vultures." She shivered.

Ella plunked down on the end of the bed, and Brita sat beside her. The smell of the fresh doughnuts made her mouth water, and Brita immediately reached for the bag.

"Wow," Brita said after a few bites, wondering if she'd died and gone to heaven. "These are really good. Thanks." She grinned before licking her lips to remove the chocolate tidbits.

"So, what can you tell me about all of this hoopla going on out here?" Ella asked. Her dark brows were raised in a question mark as she scrutinized Brita. "Well?"

"I suppose it won't hurt. At least you'll not have to depend on rumors." Brita licked her fingertips. "Rose is dead. She must've had a heart attack. She'd asked me to wake her up, and there wasn't an answer when I knocked. Dwight opened the door, we stepped inside and found her. That's all there is to it." Brita almost felt like snapping her fingers, but didn't. "I think it's safer in the military. When I'm through with this run, I'm going to join the WACS. In fact, I rather like the idea." She reached into the bag for another doughnut.

"Rose is dead?" Ella leaned back into the wall. "I don't believe it." She shook her head, and crumpled up the bag. "Well, now I know what all the hoopla is about." She stood up. "I've got sounds to perfect and knittin' to do. If you hear anything else worthwhile, just let me know, will ya?" She wiggled. "I'm all set."

"You bet," Brita said. She watched Ella straighten her shoulders before opening the door and marching into the crowd. Brita closed the door and shook her head. She glanced at her watch and realized that the morning was half gone. The sun shone bright for an autumn day, and the wind wasn't blowing quite as fiercely as it had in Chicago. The women didn't hold onto their hats as they walked down the street, and the men's long coats weren't flapping out like duck wings. Burlington was just far enough south that the trees still had a few leaves left on them.

Out of the depot door, a policeman and someone dressed in a suit and wearing a fedora walked briskly to the zephyr. The engineer stepped out from the side and sauntered toward them. They shook hands while looking over at zephyr train. The policeman and the other man stepped aside as the engineer led them to the nearest door.

An unfamiliar voice announced the next message.

Good morning from the Zephyr staff, this is Carl, the engineer. There will be a slight delay before we leave for Omaha. You're all invited to the dining car for a beverage of your choice on Burlington. Take advantage of the free coffee, or go for a walk into town and visit the beautiful city of Burlington, Iowa. Thank you.

Tears moistened Brita's eyes, and she reached for her handkerchief as someone knocked on the door.

"Yes?" she answered, opening it up.

"Are you Brita Torgerson?" The policeman stood tall like a cornstalk, and his strawberry colored hair poked out from his cap like sticks.

"Yes." Brita thought of a field of mown hay when she looked at him, and decided that it was the first time that a police officer made her feel homey.

"Miss Torgerson..."

"Brita." She opened the door wider.

"Brita. I'm Sergeant Carlson. May I come in?" His voice was soft and pleasant. "I'm sure you've been expecting me."

"Yes, of course." She stepped aside to let him enter. "I really don't know what else to say about Rose." Brita cleared her throat because she suddenly felt uncomfortable talking about a dead person. "Ron—Mr. Healy—and I waited in the room until Dwight and Stan returned." Brita watched as Sergeant Carlson wrote down the information. "What do you want to know?"

"Who was with you when you entered?" he asked softly.

"Dwight." Brita frowned, and turned toward the window. After taking a deep breath, she faced him. "Little did I know that she'd be dead. That's how we found her." Brita sniffled. "She seemed like such a nice lady."

"Yes, that's the way it goes..." He finished writing down her statement, then closed his notebook. "Where's Mr. Healy's compartment?"

"It's number seven." Brita fought back tears.

"Thank you." Sergeant Carlson let himself out.

Brita turned to the window and saw Mr. Swensen and Father O'Malley approaching the train, and she wondered if there would be time for her to go to town also. She was beginning to feel claustrophobic, and decided that fresh air would lift her spirits.

Brita stepped out into the hallway and found several people lingering by Rose's door. She decided to ask if anyone had seen Stan or Dwight because one of them was supposed to be outside Rose's door.

"Brita? What's happening? Did someone die?" Mrs. Bakko asked. "I want to know… no, I deserve to know." She crossed her arms and nodded.

"Yes, someone died, and it appears to have been a heart attack. Have you seen Stan or Dwight?" Brita answered, and hoped that she was satisfied.

"No. They must still be in the room. There's another guy in there too," a man said. He wore a bright pink and purple striped shirt and polka dot tie underneath a baby blue suit.

"Hmm," Brita said, more to herself than to anyone. She turned to walk away just as Ron and Sergeant Carlson stepped out into the hallway. Ron's eyes met hers, and they smiled at each other.

"Just a minute," Ron called. He held up his hand like a stop sign. He turned to Sergeant Carlson. "May we go into town? I think a bit of fresh air would do us both good."

"Sure, why not?" Sergeant Carlson responded as he stuck the notepad into his pocket.

Ron walked away and reached out for Brita's arm, steering her outside.

"I really should have my coat, but I think the fresh air will feel good." She was thrilled that he'd taken it upon himself to request that they go out.

"The sun will warm you up and clear your mind."

"Yes, it's been a long day."

Chapter Nine

Time seemed to slip away as they stood on the lookout point and watched the boats come and go. Riverboats and barges made their way gracefully up and down the Mississippi. The water slapped against the shoreline in a quiet rhythm, lulling the onlookers.

"How do you know that we weren't followed?" Brita yawned as she studied her surroundings.

"I don't, but I've kept a look out. No one is lurking," Ron said. He took another glance around them. "I'm ready for a good night's sleep."

"I'm still tired. It's been a long trip." She sighed, looking up at Ron. "Don't you agree?" She blinked from the sunlight.

"You bet." Ron smiled down at her. "Let's continue walking. It's good to keep moving." He took her elbow and escorted her away from the spot.

Many passengers strolled along the side of the depot. It was situated by the Mississippi River, which ran parallel with the trains. They decided to join the strollers along the boardwalk, which led up and down the riverbank. A small paddlewheel boat blew its horn, and the captain waved at the onlookers. The early afternoon sun sparkled across the dark blue autumnal water like a diamond.

Ron took her hand in his as they stopped to look back at the two-story brick depot. The railyard was quite small and limited in comparison to Chicago's. However, the quaint town—with its brick buildings nestled beside the river—held a romantic, old-world charm which captured Ron's heart.

"This town reminds me of Europe," Ron said. Suddenly he recalled his deceased fiancée, Margot, and thought of his mission… and the general.

"Me too. It's similar to smaller towns in Germany or in England. Anywhere, I guess." She smiled up at him. Walking so near to him sent ripples down her spine; it brought back memories of when she'd first fallen in love with Winston. Remembering her resolve, she dropped his hand abruptly. "Shall we walk into town?"

"There must be a small diner that serves great apple pie," Ron said. He gave her a sideways glance and shook his head.

"Sounds good," she admitted. There was a killer in their midst. Brita frowned as the memory of the knife and picture came to mind.

Closely they walked up the block and looked for a diner sign.

"I see a sign for Mel's Diner on the next block."

"You know, I think I'd rather enjoy the fresh air after being inside all day. Let's keep walking for a little while."

"Are you sure? You look pale." Ron glanced at her with a puzzled look and took her hand again.

"No, I'm fine," she whispered. She raised her eyes to meet his. "Let's keep walking. It's not too brisk, or as terribly windy as Chicago."

"You know, maybe we should head back to the Z. Just in case we're going to get rolling soon." He cleared his throat and tried to pull his eyes from hers, but found it difficult. A train whistled in the distance, which broke the mood.

"Yes. Yes, of course, you're right," Brita said, sucking in her breath. "We need to take care of the passengers who are coming on board." Brita wondered if the time was right to tell him about the knife and picture, but decided to keep it a secret until they learned the cause of Rose's death.

Ron took her elbow and guided her toward the train. As one passed, they shuddered from the whoosh of the wind while Brita held on to her hat. The leaves of the nearby trees shook loose and fell to the ground like petals. The amber, orange and red of the falling maple leaves against the sky-blue background made a scene.

"Do you think that the coroner has come and removed Rose's body?" Brita asked, looking over at him. "I hope so. I'm anxious to get to Denver and put this trip behind me. I've decided that I'm going to join the WACS. Being a Zephyrette is too hazardous to my health. I'm sure glad that I'll have my nursing skills to rely on. It's a requirement as a Zephyrette. Did you know that?"

"No. It's understandable, since there's so many passengers onboard and it's a closed environment." Ron squeezed her arm. "Here we are."

Brita stepped aside as he opened the train door, and they went inside. The lounge was filled with blue smoke rings and card players with cigar butts stuck in the corners of their mouths. Women sat behind a couple of the men, watching. In one corner, four women sat playing bridge and drinking sodas. Through the opposite window, Brita saw the back of the depot and the arrival and departure of passengers.

Men still wore suits and ties with heavy, long wool coats, but the women seemed to be more in touch with the coming ride, and weren't dressed in as fancy attire. Brita noticed less high-heeled shoes and fewer feather-bobbed hats. Babies were bundled up and wrapped in homemade comforters, which reminded Brita of her bedspread as a child. She glanced at her watch. "It's getting late. I think I'll check on the passengers before getting a bite to eat." Brita looked at Ron, who'd already stepped behind the bar. "I'm worried. How about you?"

"There are plenty of authority figures nearby to keep us safe."

"I hope you're right."

"Let's plan on dinner around seven tonight. Okay?" he asked quietly.

"It's a date." Brita replied, and felt the same tingle when he smiled at her. "I need to get busy." She didn't want to leave his side, but knew that she must.

Brita kept walking until she reached the dining car. She

found Gladys sitting and sipping on a root beer.

"I'm heading up to the observation deck. It doesn't look like you need any help in here," Brita said. "I just returned from a walk and the fresh air felt good."

"You betcha. Just got in from a bit of a walk myself. Had to get outta here, you know?" Gladys took a quick sip. "Have a seat. It won't be long and we'll be up and rolling and then you won't get a chance." She took another swallow, and smacked her lips. "Mighty good."

"I will in a little while. See you later." Brita left the dining car.

Not many passengers were in the observation deck. The few that she saw were relaxing and reading or talking with a partner, so she decided to leave. On her way back through the lounge, Brita noticed that Ron was busy serving up drinks and beers to the passengers. Swensen and Jacques were rolling dice, and they called her name in unison.

"Want another drink?" Brita asked, going over to them. She could tell by their bleary eyes that they'd been drinking all afternoon. "Where's Carlo?"

"He got off as soon as the train stopped," Jacques said, then hiccupped. "How about another round?"

"Hey, you ever been to the Orpheum and seen the Marx Brothers? They sure are somethin'," Swensen slurred. "Here, the drinks are on me."

"Can't say as I have." Brita took the money and walked to the bar.

"Here," she said to Ron. "Take them their usual, I've got work to do. I don't plan to spend my time with two sots." She shrugged.

"Okay. See you later." Ron winked. He began filling the order as she walked away.

As Brita entered the larger sitting car, the passengers seemed to be dozing in their seats or reading. It made her life easier that they were all content. When Brita entered the vestibule and stepped into the corridor of the next car, she stopped and looked toward the town of Burlington.

The clock tower on a distant brick building was stunning, and Brita wished that they'd had the chance to walk farther into town. Shoppers walked in and out of stores carrying packages. Paved roads extended from the depot all the way up into town, and eventually turned to gravel. A few horses dotted the streets alongside the cars. A tractor pulling a hayrack was sputtering off in another direction. A grain elevator stood in the distance, and she figured that was where the farmer was heading. The silver Zephyr would shine like a ribbon beside the road and into the prairie. Brita couldn't wait to get started again.

Her thoughts went to Ron, and she decided to just think of him as a dear friend. It didn't matter that he made her nerves tingle or her heart jump… because when the trip was over, he'd only bring her more heartache.

The door opened behind her, and Brita looked back. It was Father O'Malley. When their eyes met, Brita shivered as if a cold north wind had blown up her spine.

"Brita, isn't it? Aren't you the one who found poor Rose's body this morning?"

"Yes, Father." Brita nodded.

"Weren't you involved in another death in Chicago as well?" he accused.

"Ah, not exactly involved. More of just a witness… sort of," Brita stammered against his piercing gaze. His cold eyes made her shiver.

"Perhaps a blessing from the Lord can protect you from further contact from the devil." Raising the crucifix that hung from his neck with his right hand, he blessed her, then began to walk away.

"Thank you," she whispered. Brita hugged herself from his frigid stare and wondered… then admonished herself because he was a man of God, and it wasn't possible that he could be a murderer. But weren't those terribly cold eyes unusual for a man of the cloth?

After he'd exited, Brita started toward the sleeping car.

Rose's compartment was still closed, so she decided to stop and speak with Dwight.

"When will the train start up again? I don't see any new passengers coming onboard," Brita said. She looked down at what he was writing on the time record.

"I haven't heard anything yet," Dwight said. He set aside the record and his pencil. "It seems like a long time, but the police have left and they've removed Rose's body." He sighed and yawned. "I wish this day was over."

"Me, too. So, we're just waiting for the go-ahead?" Brita crossed her arms and leaned on the nearest door. "I'm tired, I'm hungry, and I feel like I'm going to bust if we don't start moving pretty soon." Brita yawned.

"I'll let you in on any news," Dwight said. He placed the record back in the wall slot.

While Brita continued to her destination, she thought about the length of time since Rose was found. It seemed like they should've left Burlington by now. She couldn't understand what was taking so long, but reasoned that it was a small town, and everything took longer because of it.

Mounting the stairs into the observation deck, she saw farmland for as far as the eye could see. Farmers with corn pickers were out in the fields harvesting. In Minnesota, the farmers had already harvested and brought in their yield. The difference in the weather was amazing to her. A flag flew on top of a large brick building that looked like a courthouse because of the size of the rotunda. She glanced across to the watchtower and realized that it was the famed library. Brita made a mental note to visit that building if she ever got the chance, because it looked spectacular. The quaintness of the river town sparked her interest.

Sitting to the side were two women with their children. Brita walked over to them. "How are you doing? Do you need anything? Is there something I can help you with?" Brita asked. The babies were sound asleep and the mothers were making dolls from socks to play with as toys.

"That's quite all right," one responded. She gave Brita a smile. "Here," she said to her little girl.

"How cute," Brita replied.

As her eyes skimmed the passengers, she tried to see who might need assistance, when Ella's head bobbed up from the side window. Brita walked over to her.

"Are you going to be knitting?" Brita noticed that now she had wooden blocks on her lap and grinned, knowing that it was a dumb question.

"Nope. I heard a faint sound last night, and I'm trying to duplicate it." Ella knocked two blocks softly together. "Not right, yet." She shook her head.

As soon as the announcers voice blared, and it appeared as if everyone sat straighter.

This is Stan, the conductor. It is four o'clock in the afternoon. We will be overnight in Burlington. I hope that we will begin our journey to Omaha at daybreak. Until further notice, this is where we'll be staying. Brita Torgerson and Ron Healy, you are to go directly to your compartments. Over and out.

After serving the last customer, Ron looked up and saw Harold walking toward him.

"I'm taking over for you until your return. The dining car will have to be closed for a short time anyway, because we're running out of food." Harold moved aside to let Ron out and touched his hand. "Don't fret. I've been a bartender before, in my other single life." He grinned, and his teeth sparkled white in contrast to his dark skin.

"Good. I feel better," Ron said, annoyed. "This is troublesome, don't you think?" He raised his brow and cocked his head, waiting for an answer.

"Nah. The police are just doing their job," Harold answered consolingly. "Don't give it another thought." He stepped behind the bar and looked up as a customer approached.

"See you later." Ron walked away from the bar, resigned.

As Ron headed toward his compartment, he wondered why there would be more questioning. He'd spent the last couple of hours trying to sort out a common thread between Mindel and Rose, but couldn't. The only factor that might play well would be if they knew each other, but that still made no sense at all to him.

As he passed through the many vestibules and corridors, he noticed that the sun was beginning to set, and frowned. He wished that the Burlington contact would reach out to him soon. It irritated him, not knowing about the necktie knot. To make matters worse, Brita's charm and beauty had gotten under his skin, which was worrisome since her life was probably in danger. *Stay sharp and alert,* he scolded himself. *Don't act like a teenager in heat.*

Ron opened his compartment door and entered, locking it behind him. He slumped down onto his bed and reached for his notepad and pen.

He wrote Rose and Mindel's names at the top of the page, and drew a line down between them. Besides the fact that they were similar in age and had both ridden on the Twin Cities Z, they hadn't anything else in common. Ron couldn't recall ever seeing them speak to each other in the lounge car, which brought him back full circle to the present time. The police were keeping the train from leaving, so he had to have been correct. Her death wasn't natural.

He stared out the window and hoped that every new male he saw approaching the train would end up being his contact.

As he watched the passersby, Ron noticed there were several young police officers taking notes from the various railyard men. One man stood rolling a stogie around in his mouth like an extension of his tongue. Another officer interviewed a yard man who stuck a wad of tobacco in his mouth, and then spit on the ground like he was doing target practice.

Ron noticed Sergeant Carlson and another fellow in a suit and fedora exit the depot and walk swiftly to the train. He hoped that the contact was the man wearing the fedora.

The light knock on his door caught Ron's attention, and he turned. "Yes?" He was sure that he was being summoned. No one answered, and he looked to the floor and found a note. It read:

Mel's diner. Six PM.

Ron ripped up the paper and stuck sections of it in each of his pockets for later disposal at various sites. He didn't want anyone to be able to put the words together, because of the secrecy of the request. He looked up at another knock on the door.

"Mr. Healy?" the caller said, with authority.

"Yes?" Ron answered, opening up. "Sergeant Carlson, I see. Back again?" Ron raised a brow in question and crossed his arms.

"Come with me, sir," Sergeant Carlson ordered, and stepped aside for Ron. When the door shut, they started walking.

"The station master wants to ask a few questions of you and Miss Torgerson, before we can let the train go." The sergeant stopped outside of Rose's door. "Here we are." He opened the door and stepped aside.

The man wearing the fedora looked up from Rose's bed as Ron entered. Their eyes met.

"Sir?" Ron took a minute to study him. He wore oversized dark glasses that balanced on a pert little nose. His beady eyes and tousled hair gave him the appearance of a squirrel.

"Mr. Healy?" the man asked, stepping back. He studied Ron. After a moment, he said, "I'm the station master, Mr. Sloan, and I'm wondering what you saw when you entered this compartment. Does it look like anything has been moved? Did you see anything or anyone outside of her compartment, or giving her extra attention yesterday?" He cleared his throat and kept his eyes glued on Ron.

"The newspaper was on the counter, and her makeup was sitting out also. Like this." Ron rearranged the few pieces to the way that they were at the time he entered the compartment. It was unusual, but he reckoned that each investigator had his own way of making sure that suspects weren't lying.

"Can you tell me anything else? Anything that hasn't been told already?" the man asked, keeping his smile thin as he appeared to watch Ron for any sign of nervousness.

"No. I was in the lounge all day working, and had dinner with Brita. She found the body, not me, and it was about 6:30 this morning. I picked up that streetcar token and handed it to Stan. I really don't know anything else." Ron shrugged, crossed his arms and leaned into the wall.

"Do you know when the train stopped in Burlington, or how long it was delayed before it entered the yard?"

"Not really, no. Why haven't you asked Stan or the engineer?" Ron stared at him, slightly annoyed. He suppressed a yawn. "It's nearly six, and I need fresh air. If there's nothing else, can I go to town for a short walk?"

"Sure. We'll be here all night, and in the morning we'll decide what to do." Mr. Sloan glanced at his watch. "Thank you. Don't be gone long in case I have any other questions. I want to get this wrapped up right away."

"Sure. I understand." Ron placed his hand on the doorknob and was about to walk out when Mr. Sloan stopped him with another question.

"By the way… when was the last time you were in Seattle?"

"Before the war broke out. I was visiting my mother. Why do you ask?" Ron cocked his head to the side and studied Sloan.

"Just curious." Mr. Sloan's eyes met Ron's for a few brief moments. "One more thing…"

"And that is?" Ron asked, slightly annoyed by the stopping and starting of the questioning.

"When you were held over in Chicago, did you see anyone lurking about? Did you see anyone enter the train who wasn't a passenger?" He peered at Ron.

"Not that I can recall, but I suspect that it's possible. The train is awfully long, and I don't get out beyond the bar much.

Is that all?" Ron clamped his jaw tight to prevent himself from saying something that he shouldn't.

"You may go now." Mr. Sloan finished writing in his notepad.

"Thanks." Ron headed out the door and noticed that Stan was just leaving Brita's compartment. Ron hesitated, hoping that she'd wait a second before walking out, because he wanted to reassure her about the questioning.

Brita's door slowly opened, and he walked directly to it.

"You're next?" Ron couldn't pull his gaze from her beautiful eyes. When she nodded, he tried to make her feel better. "It's the station master." He reached for her hand and squeezed it.

"Thank you. I have to go now." Brita pulled back her hand.

Rose's door opened, and Mr. Sloan stepped out. "Miss Torgerson? I'm waiting." He held the door open for her.

As Ron crossed through the cars and headed for the side door—which wasn't near the lounge because he didn't want to be seen by Harold—his thoughts went to the streetcar token. It was unusual for the streetcar token to be from Seattle, because most of the passengers were from Minnesota, Wisconsin, or Illinois.

Ron tried to shake the suspicion that both deaths were connected as he entered Mel's Diner, the place he remembered from his walkabout with Brita.

*****

Brita walked out of Rose's compartment, completely in a muddle. While rearranging the room as it had been, Brita thought that Mr. Sloan was trying to trick her… and then when he asked about Seattle, she knew he was. Because how could Seattle have anything to do with Rose's death? Brita became more puzzled because Ron was the only person that she knew who came from Seattle. Rose had suffered a heart attack, she was positive.

Brita shook off her suspicions and stopped for a minute to look outside. Burlington was pretty. She looked toward the town, and saw the flags out front of the store windows being lowered or taken off their spindles. Last minute shoppers hustled to their cars and trucks. Even though it was a smaller town compared to Minneapolis, the streets bustled just as much. After a few more minutes of watching the quaint community, a train whistled its approach, and Brita turned away.

When she entered the parlor car, Brita found it full of children and three young mothers, plus Ella.

"Ella? What a pleasant surprise." Brita smiled as she looked at the young mothers. "I'm Brita. Can I get anyone a cup of tea or coffee? Maybe a cookie for the little ones?" She gave Ella a questioning look.

"I came in here to make some rag dolls for the babies. It seems that because of the hold over, we're stuck here for a while and the kids were getting bored and restless. I volunteered my services." She held up a floppy doll made from fabric scraps. Opening her bag, she removed small blocks, a toy alarm clock, and jingle bells, which she shook. She put a whistle to her mouth, but stopped when Brita shook her head. "Oh, sure… it'll scare the kids. Should've known." Ella stuck the whistle back in her bag.

"Right. You're good entertainment," Brita said, chuckling. "I wish that you had been my next-door neighbor or grandma. We would've had a great time."

"I have many new friends. This is Molly and her daughter, Amy." Ella nodded to her. "And Sandy, Brian and Keith. And let's see… Inga. Right? And then, let's see…Magdalene."

"Have you been on many radio shows?" Molly asked. "I listen to Burns and Allen all the time, and the *Amos 'n' Andy* show. I just love them."

"I circle around. I'm good at finding places and fitting in because I keep up with new sounds." Ella bopped the block down on a piece of fabric, and frowned.

"My husband likes *The Shadow*," Magdalene said, nodding to herself as she rocked the baby.

"Oh yeah, that's a popular one too," Ella replied. "Here's another doll." She held it up. "Wait a second here." She took a small block, wrapped it in a piece of fabric and dropped it. "I almost got it." She shook her head.

"What?" Brita asked. She moved closer to Ella to take a quick glance inside of the bag. "You still trying to figure out that sound from last night?"

"Yep. I won't quit till I do. I might need it for one of my shows."

"What sound would you use it for?" Brita wondered, amazed at the combination of items used to duplicate different sounds and effects.

"Not sure, but I'll figure something out. Too bad I was just dozing off when I heard it. Oh well." She glanced at the kids. "Want another doll?"

"Since I have no takers for tea or coffee, I'll move on. Enjoy yourself."

Brita walked out the door.

Stan's voice came on the public address system to deliver a message.

Due to unforeseen difficulties and food shortages, this evening's menu has been changed. Instead of prime roast beef, it will be chicken. The vegetables will be carrots, grown from the local farmers, instead of potatoes.

Tomorrow morning we will be refilling the freezers and will be starting later than usual. Over and out.

*****

No one besides the employees were in Mel's Diner as Ron slid into an empty booth. The waitress came over, and he ordered a fried egg sandwich and a cup of coffee. It felt good to be on his own and away from the train and its passengers. To his relief, he realized that being away from Brita also helped him to think more clearly.

Brita had captured his mind, and made his imagination run completely wild. All he could think about was being with her;

he hadn't felt as absorbed with a woman before, and it astounded him. He hadn't been able to fall asleep last night, because of guilt over Margot. He'd cursed himself for taking on the assignment before he finally closed his eyes.

Ron looked up as the little bell above the diner door jingled. A man wearing a nondescript brown suit, tie, and hat entered. Their eyes met, and Ron wondered if it was the contact. At the same time, a man dressed as a minister walked in and glanced at Ron. Reaching for his red handkerchief, Ron blew his nose as a signal. Neither of the men approached.

The waitress brought over the sandwich and coffee. Ron relaxed and began to eat his meal.

After he'd finished, Ron glanced at his watch. It read 6:15. He wondered what he should do. Since he'd thrown the message away, he couldn't reread it. Doubts about the time and place swarmed his mind, until at last the bell jingled again and someone else entered. The man wore bib overalls and barn boots, with a feed cap perched on top of his head. A toothpick poked out of his mouth as he took a gander around the room.

Ron removed his handkerchief and blew his nose. The man walked over to join him.

"Hey cuz, how ya been?" he said. As he crawled into the booth opposite Ron, he chewed on the toothpick. "You look tired."

"I am," Ron said. "How's that for a flashy answer?" He yawned, and wondered if the guy really was the agent. Giving him a closer scrutiny, Ron asked, "What do you know about tying knots?" Ron thought the guy looked like he just fell from a threshing machine.

"It's like this." He leaned closer and whispered, "I've been sent to answer your question about tying ties."

"And?" Ron said, puzzled.

"The knot was a slip knot with the back link pulled back through, making it a double knot instead of a necktie. Impossible to untangle in the dark unless you were looking for it." The man shook his head to the waitress who held up an empty coffee cup. "No thanks, Mildred. I'm just saying 'hey' to a cousin." He turned to Ron and said, "Any more questions? I have to get moving. Mildred's the town's rumor mill." He winked before breaking off the end of the toothpick.

"I understand. Could this killer, in your estimation, know how to use a tie as a weapon beyond the usual Windsor knot? Would he be that much of an expert?" Ron admired the agent's costume, because he found it hard to believe that this common person was an OSS agent.

"Let's put it like this… anyone who would know how to tie a knot like that would know what he was doing. Does that answer your question?" the man said, sliding to the end. "Done?"

"One more. What do you know about a Dr. Charlot Fortier? He was missing at the time of my reassignment."

"His body was found at the Illinois border, near the tracks. Poisoned and tossed out with his suitcase like cattle fodder." The agent reached for a new toothpick.

"Any suspects?"

"Not besides the Nazi killer who is still on the loose." He stuck the toothpick in his mouth.

"That explains why the train wasn't detained any longer," Ron said.

"Anything else?"

"Done, and thanks. I've got the information that I need." Ron nodded, then gave the man a quick smile.

The man got up and strode right out the door. Ron kept his eyes on him and watched as he walked over to an old Ford truck and piled inside of it. The box was heaped high with hay bales.

Ron took a moment to sip the rest of his coffee and let his mind go over what he'd just learned. Since he couldn't link Mindel and Margot's murder, Ron wasn't sure if it was the same killer. Fortier was poisoned, for unknown reasons. Rose's death needed to be investigated to make sure that it wasn't from natural causes. The Nazi was shot in Chicago. Nothing added up.

Shaking his head, Ron sat the empty cup down and left the restaurant.

Who could be the next victim?

Chapter Ten

Ron kept his eyes open for any suspicious characters as he hiked back to the train. He thought of the goose-stepping German soldiers and pondered any recent passengers with possible accents.

Stars were beginning to dot the sky as he entered the two-story brick depot. The inside wasn't swarmed with a massive number of passengers as it had been in Chicago, and Ron felt a comfortable pleasure from that. The women passengers looked quaint in homemade dresses, and the men wore shirts and dress slacks. Ron felt as if he'd stepped into the past.

As he crossed through the main reception room, he happened to see Mr. Sloan speaking to another railroad man. Ron decided to go over to them because he wanted to know if the investigation was over, and what their findings were.

The bull had the same features as the agent he'd just spoken to in the diner. He had a stogie sticking out from the side of his mouth… and he had a knack of chewing it while speaking at the same time. With a start, Ron realized that he was the same person that he'd just met with. When Ron drew closer, their eyes met and held. Ron swallowed and took a deep breath as he came to stop right beside them.

"Ron Healy, this is the yard bull, Ole Ferguson. He was working last night," Mr. Sloan said, glancing from one to the other. "He's been a hard one to track down. His farm is out in the country, of course. It's threshing and harvesting time, so he works late hours here in the yard after pulling in a full day at home. So we're just now getting to talk."

"Sure. That's how it is sometimes," Ron conceded with a nod. Learning more about Ole helped him feel more secure in the answers that he'd been given. "Farming is hard work, and then to come here… it must keep you busy."

Ole nodded.

"I'm just finishing my questioning. I'll make up my report later tonight, then get it sent off to my superiors," Mr. Sloan explained As he finished tucking his notepad inside of his pocket. "In the morning, we'll hear from Burlington and find out if the train will be allowed to continue on its journey."

"I'm glad," Ron responded with relief. "I was wondering, why is there an investigation, since Rose appeared to have died from a heart attack? It seems to be taking forever." He looked at Sloan point blank, studying him before glancing at Ole. "What's going on?"

"There was something about her that made the coroner contact me," Mr. Sloan said with a frown. "Rose was murdered, but we think it was done by someone who sneaked on during the night and has since jumped aboard another train. We have a brief description of a man who was removed from another train for drunkenness during the night, and we think it was him." He raised his brow and crossed his arms as studied Ron.

"Do you have a name?" Ron asked.

"No, but he was of medium build, with fair skin and short brown hair."

"Did you know that we've already had a murder?" Ron was beginning to wonder if Sloan knew anything at all, or if he was just trying to pass the investigation onto someone else. "It was a passenger who'd been on the train from the Twin Cities to Chicago. He was found on the tracks, and the description of the murderer is the same."

"I'm not so sure that they're not related. They're similar since both murders happened on or near a train." Ron raised his brow and stared at Sloan. "It's very possible," Sloan said.

"What happened to Rose?" Ole asked.

"Her neck was broken. There was something else found as well, but I'm not at liberty to say what it was." Sloan hesitated and rubbed his chin before shaking his head. "The thing was found in her mouth."

"I didn't know that there'd been another murder," Ole replied. He took a moment to try to decide how to proceed. He took a silver dollar out of his pocket and flipped it in the air. "I must get back to work." He strode away, still flipping the coin.

"Me, too," Mr. Sloan said with an annoyed look toward Ole.

As Ron walked out of the depot and headed toward the train, he mulled over the fact that Rose had definitely been murdered. He drew in a deep breath as he finished walking to the Zephyr. The murders were too coincidental and happening too close together. Rose's death didn't make any sense to him.

Reluctantly, he stepped inside the lounge car and went back to his post as a bartender. He hoped that he'd have time to speak with Brita. With any luck, they could figure out more about Rose before the sunrise.

*****

Brita had been busy scurrying back and forth and up and down and all over, taking care of irate passengers. They moaned and groaned because they thought that by riding the Zephyr, they'd get to Omaha or Denver faster. They hadn't planned to be waylaid by one death after another. "It's a shame. I'm so sorry for the person and families," she answered over and over. She wanted to hide in her room with a pillow pulled over her head.

It was just by luck that Brita happened to be in the same coach when Ron walked in, looking quite gloomy. She walked over to him.

"I've missed you. Where have you been? Harold wasn't nearly as good at serving drinks as you." Brita gave him a lighthearted smile. When he looked into her eyes, she felt her heart skip a beat.

"I just found out some bad news," he said softly. "We need to talk later. In the meantime, can you think about all the passengers that you might have seen Rose speaking to?" He reached for her hand. "Please don't mention this to anyone just yet."

"This doesn't sound good. It sounds too much like the last time. Don't tell me that she was murdered too?" When he nodded, tears sprang into her eyes. "Okay, I'll do my best to investigate, and then we'll compare notes. I'll keep it a secret." Her heart fluttered and her fingers felt warm after he'd removed his hand.

"Thanks." Ron looked up as a customer wearing a fedora, striped shirt and baggy suit approached, waving an empty beer bottle. "Another? Mr. — ?"

"Tennyson. Call me Mark. Yep, I'd like another one," he answered. He set the empty bottle on the counter and smacked his lips.

Brita walked away.

"Wow!" Mark took the bottle. "Thanks." He slapped the money down and walked back to the poker table.

Ron noticed that each and every one of the men smoked cigars, pipes, or cigarettes, and the good-looking ones had women hovering over them. Swensen and Jacques, per usual, were in the thick of it, and had several empty beer bottles in front of them. He grinned to himself and went back to washing the glasses.

Brita wondered how Rose was murdered as she hiked to the observation deck. She'd just stopped for a moment with Gladys, and she hadn't said anything about a murder. Brita concluded that she and Ron were the only people who knew about Rose. The fewer people who knew, the better off everyone would be.

Her mind went back to Mindel, and then to Rose. She still couldn't connect the murders. Brita was starting to think that maybe she'd been going about everything wrong. Maybe they had too much in common… but still she couldn't see how it was possible. Then there was the return of her knife with a hole right through Charlot's picture. Her dear, sweet friend and godfather. Brita couldn't see any connection between the murders except for the friendship through her father—but how could he know Rose?

Stop, she admonished herself. She was going to drive herself crazy with worry. Deep down, however, Brita knew she was the connecting link. *The murderer must have fled*, she reassured herself while climbing the stairs.

When Brita reached the top of the observation deck, she took the moment to look out. The sun had dropped, and the moon was casting its silver rays like a blanket across the glistening river.

The observation deck was pretty empty; there were only a few older gentlemen reading the paper. Brita decided that most people had either left the Zephyr for another train, or they were in the dining car eating.

Brita sat for a moment and let her thoughts wander. She turned over everything that Mr. Sloan had asked and what she'd known about Rose in her mind. She had an uneasy feeling in her gut that couldn't be brushed aside.

Why did Rose have to be murdered? That was the question that troubled her most. Sighing, she closed her eyes and recalled the last few words that had been spoken between her and Rose. They had been simple… just the request to check on her in the morning. Brita realized that, unfortunately, she was going to have to ask Gladys a few questions.

Brita wasn't exactly sure where to find Gladys, but guessed that she hadn't left the train. A smile tugged the corners of her mouth as she climbed down the back stairs.

As she passed through the coaches and came into her own, Brita decided to stop by Dwight's desk.

"Brita." Dwight looked up at her as she entered, and smiled. "You look troubled," he said, concerned. "What's on your mind?" He flipped up his black hat, smoothed down his hair and set the hat back down.

"I miss Rose, even though I really didn't know her," Brita said, sniffling. She blew her nose. "I don't recall her ever saying anyone's name, or sitting with anyone. How about you?"

Leaning on the next door, she sighed. "Do you know, did she have any friends on the train that might need extra comfort or attention?"

"Hmm, let me think on this." Dwight rubbed his chin. "I didn't see her go into her compartment because I was helping Ella with her key. She couldn't see well enough, and with the rocking motion of the train, she couldn't slip it into the keyhole." He raised a puzzled brow and continued rubbing his chin.

"What? You look like you might remember something." Brita crossed her arms. "I feel so bad for Rose… I wonder if she had a family."

"So many people walk through this corridor to go up to the observation deck that anyone could've come through and I wouldn't have known it. I don't pay much attention unless something strikes me as odd. There wasn't anything last night that did." He raised his soft brown eyes. "I'm sorry—I'm not much help."

"That's fine." Brita shrugged. "I'm just going to have to forget about it."

As she walked down the corridor and out into the vestibule, Brita heaved a long sigh and wished that she were someplace else. When passing by the long window spans, she noticed a lone tree in the distance with the moon perched on top like a huge silver globe.

Brita wondered as she walked if Ella ever spoke with Rose, and decided that it was possible.

Ron was busy serving drinks to several customers when Brita entered. He raised his finger as a signal to her, and smiled when she walked over to him.

"I'm ready for a break. How about you?" he whispered. "How about if we find a quiet place to sit?"

"I'm sort of hungry, actually. I'll see if I can get Harold to make me a sandwich. There are very few people in the observation deck." She held her breath in anticipation of his answer.

"Good idea, but we'd better leave separately. When I see you go by with a little lunch bag, I'll follow about ten minutes later. What do you want to drink?" He held his breath as he gazed into her beautiful eyes, and his fingers tingled.

"Root beer. See you in a bit," she replied, winking.

Brita sashayed away, knowing that he was watching. A ripple of excitement coursed through her veins, which made her shiver. She longed to just sit beside him without anyone near.

*****

When Ron watched her as she walked away, his heart leapt. He gulped, and wished he'd never taken the job. Romance was finding him, and he was ill-equipped to handle it at present.

After a quick glance at his watch, Ron picked up the bar rag and began wiping down the counter top. He moved around to the various booths. Two couples were busy playing a game of cards, and one of the men held up his finger for another round of drinks.

"Will do," Ron called. He shifted gears and went back to the bar and poured two brandy and waters for the men, and opened two bottles of 7 Up for the women.

"Here you are." Ron placed the drinks on the table, then thanked the customers when they handed him the money.

Ron picked up his rag again and went to the table that had the most empty beer bottles on it. Swensen was passed out like a light, and snoring. Father O'Malley walked into the room and glanced over to Ron.

"Another fallen soldier," Father O'Malley preached.

With his arms full of empty beer bottles, Ron returned to the bar and deposited them in their respective cases. He looked up as Mark Tennyson, the man he'd met earlier, held up an empty bottle. Ron put the money in the till and reached for a full one. He brought the beer over to Mark.

"Here," Ron said. He took the money and put it in the till. Brita must be passing through soon, he hoped, and looked at his watch again. He was anxious to leave.

Ron walked back to the bar.

He continued wiping the counter and washing the glasses, but his mind went over what the bull, Ole, had done with the silver dollar. For an agent, it was an odd thing for him to do, swinging the streetcar token. The silver dollar meant something. There was no other explanation, Ron reasoned. He glanced up and saw Brita passing with a small bag in hand, and he quickly looked at his watch. It was seven-thirty.

A customer came to the counter and Ron fixed him a gin and tonic. After the customer had left, Ron placed the rag under the counter and reached for two root beer sodas. He headed out the door.

Ron tried his best to slow his heartbeat down—and his feet— but couldn't. He couldn't wait to sit with her again, hopefully alone this time.

*****

Brita found two chairs off to the side where the view wasn't as good. The deck was almost empty. When she'd entered, the last two gentlemen stood up and left, as if she were disturbing them. She was happy to see them go, because all that she could think about was being alone with Ron.

As she opened the bag, her stomach began growling. She knew it was ungracious of her and she should wait for Ron, but she was too hungry. The crisp lettuce, juicy tomato slices, pickles, and chicken piled between the fresh bread made her think of a Dagwood sandwich. When she heard the footsteps on the stairs, Brita turned to look. A smile the size of Cupid's bow crossed her face. She raised her arm to catch his attention. When he smiled, Brita's heart skipped a beat.

"Back in the corner, I see." Ron sat down beside her. "Your perfume smells like roses. Nice." He looked at her sandwich. "I should've had you get one for me, too

"Here, I brought you a piece of fresh apple pie." She exchanged his pie for the root beer. Their fingers touched, and her eyes opened wider. "This is fun, isn't it?"

"Meeting like this? You bet. I get tired of being around all those people. Don't you?" He took a bite of the pie and smiled. "This is the best pie I've ever tasted." He took a swallow of his root beer.

Brita continued eating and drinking her soda, barely tasting the food. All that was on her mind was his nearness, and how good it felt to be next to him. Her heart seemed to flip-flop with each breath, and it was getting harder and harder to swallow her food.

"What do you think about Rose being murdered?" Ron asked. "I'm pretty certain that a passenger did it." He waited as Brita finished her sandwich.

"You might be right," Brita said. "However, when was the last time that you were in Seattle?" Brita stared at him.

"Not for years. I haven't a clue how that token ended up in her room, if that's what you're wondering. Remember? I picked it up from the floor," he said, cocking his head.

"It doesn't make sense. It's not likely Rose's, is it? So maybe it came from the killer," she conceded. "Any ideas?" She rubbed her chin, she looked at him. "I wish that we could make sense of the situation."

"I have a few theories about that. Let me ask you a question." He took a moment to think. "When you looked at her neck, you saw that she wore thick makeup over a birthmark. Did you happen to notice if there was a ring around her neck… like a tight necklace?" He placed his arm over the seat and settled it across her shoulders. "Think hard."

Brita placed the wrapper inside of the bag and folded it before taking a drink. She looked away for a moment and turned back to Ron.

"I can't really think of anything. Her collar was up high, so that would conceal any smears. However, the makeup smudge was about an inch wide, which is odd. It was as if someone had rubbed it afterwards." She tightened her mouth.

"Thank you, you've given me something to consider.

Anything else?" She held her breath as if he might kiss her, then he didn't.

"No, not really. Ella said she heard something and is trying to figure out what the sound was. That's all." Brita shook her head slightly.

"Interesting. That's right, she does sound for radio programs. I think I'll have a talk with her." He leaned closer to Brita. "I think we've talked enough about unpleasant matters," he said softly.

"Me, too." Brita shivered as his hot breath touched her cheek.

Ron slid his hand behind her neck, pulling her closer, and gently kissed her.

Chapter Eleven

Brita's heart fluttered as their kiss deepened. Suddenly, her eyes flashed open.

"Ouch," she said, pulling back. "What are you doing?" Her breath came hot and in short spurts while she stared into his eyes.

"Nothing. Just trying to move the armrest," Ron said reassuringly.

He placed his hand on the back of her head as she nuzzled into the crook of his neck. Placing tiny kisses on her neck and ears, he told her how beautiful she was. When he held her cheeks between his palms, he kissed her sweet-tasting lips softly at first, then more boldly.

Brita wrapped her arms around him and pressed harder and firmer into his mouth. His hot breath made her want him more, and she pulled him closer.

Ron's ears perked up at the sound of someone whistling as they climbed the observation deck stairs. Brita's eyes opened wide, and she slid down so that no one could see her.

Brita's breath caught as she waited for Ron's signal before sitting back up on the seat.

"He's gone," Ron whispered, touching her shoulder.

"Thank God it wasn't Gladys. If she saw us, there'd be no end to the rumors." She planted herself back on the seat.

"Now where were we? Oh yes…" He enveloped her in his arms and kissed her softly, then harder as his hands slid down her back and back up to her neck. He traced a line down her sides and stopped at her breasts. He kissed her again, deeper.

Brita pulled back, and stared into his eyes before returning the kiss.

"Ron," she whispered. Her heart beat strong and hard, almost choking her.

Ron pulled back.

"Brita," he whispered. He stared into her eyes and felt like he was swimming. "I'm sorry. I didn't mean for it to go this far." He held her close and listened to her beating heart.

"I… ah… me too." She pulled away from his embrace. "It's too soon." In her heart, Brita willed him to kiss her again. Her breath came in short spurts, and it was hard to remain calm when all she wanted to do was kiss him. "Ron." She looked deeply into his eyes. "We barely know each other."

Ron raised her fingers to his lips and he kissed them. "I'm sorry. You're right." He placed his arm around her shoulders and held her tight. "I'm going to have trouble restraining myself. You feel sweet, like a kitty nuzzling into my chest."

The general's warning entered his mind.

"Kiss me again," Brita whispered.

"Nope. We'd better keep this just the way it is. Friends. It's better that way," Ron said. He gulped, removing his arm from around her shoulder.

A riverboat whistled in the distance, and a train clacked across the rails, making a whooshing sound as it passed.

"I… ah… I think that I should get back to work." Brita sighed.

"Yeah. Right. Me too," Ron murmured. "I'd better go…" He stood up and was ready to walk away.

"Umm… yes," Brita agreed. He went from hot to cold in the blink of an eye, and she couldn't figure out why. It seemed like an effort when he reached down to take her hand and help her stand. "No thanks. Here." She handed him the soda bottles, and grouched. "I'll grab the rest."

*****

As Ron walked away, he prided himself on keeping his wits and not getting too intimate. It was too close, and he knew that he'd better not kiss her, touch her, or look into her eyes again.

Otherwise he'd be doomed. There'd be no way on earth that he'd ever be able to keep his hands off her if they kissed again. Then the general would kill him.

Keep your mind on the killer, Ron told himself as he marched down the steps and into the corridor. He felt like a heel for leaving Brita behind, and slowed down for her to catch up. When he heard her coming, Ron stopped completely.

"Oh. I thought you'd be well on your way," Brita said sharply. She straightened her shoulders and held her head high. "What did you want?"

"To apologize for walking out on you. I... just found myself... well... I'm sorry." He lowered his eyes and gave her a sad look. "Please forgive me for being so rude." He reached for the empty bag. "Let me throw it away. I already have the soda bottles, so it won't be a bother. It'll be my pleasure." He gave her a smile when she passed it to him. "Apology accepted?"

"Oh, all right," she said begrudgingly. "I see some lipstick. Just a minute. Can you lean down?" She reached into her pocket and drew out a handkerchief. She licked it delicately, and wiped off the smudged lipstick on his chin and right cheek. "There. That's much better."

"How's this cheek?" Ron turned his left cheek. He gave her a wicked grin when she wiped the lipstick from it. "Thank you." He kissed her forehead softly.

"You're welcome," she said matter-of-factly. She stuck the handkerchief back inside of her pocket. "I must get busy and finish up for the evening. Good night." Brita rushed away from him before he could reach out and lay his warm hand on her.

Brita listened to the overhead speaker as she walked.

This is Stan, your conductor, with the latest news. It seems that the food trucks won't make it here to deliver until tomorrow morning. There's a food shortage because of the troops. The government is holding back until their orders are met. We don't want our soldiers to starve. After the food is loaded, we will roll once again.

This will be a free night stay on Burlington. Enjoy your evening. Over and out.

The train will never make its destination, Brita grumbled to herself. First the two deaths, and now the food situation—which meant that she'd have to see Ron one extra day. She shivered and clutched her stomach as it flip-flopped. Her heart seemed to skip a beat just from the thought of him. Brita slowed down to look out at the river.

The white paint on a riverboat glistened against the moon's rays, and the lights shone bright through the windows. She could see people's shadows in the windows, and wished that she were there, too. The river gave her a sense of peace and calm, and she smiled as she reflected on the past hour with Ron.

He delighted her. His kisses sent her soaring and his lips were warm and sensual. Brita knew from her admission that she must stay away from him, or at least keep her emotions in check. She was through with love.

When Brita heard his approaching footsteps, she glanced at her watch. It was nine o'clock, and she decided that it was time to check up on Ella.

As she stood knocking on Ella's door, Ron entered the corridor.

Ron slowly walked. This assignment had been the most perplexing and difficult ever, because of the number of unanswered questions. It was hard to know how to remain professional while being infatuated with the general's daughter. When he saw her up ahead, he decided to apologize again for being such a heel.

"Brita," he said softly, touching her arm. "Please, let's start out again, shall we?"

"I'd like that, but only as friends. Okay?" She arched her brow.

"Sure. If we end up being stuck here until later, let's go for a walk in town." He held his breath as he waited for her answer.

"Agreed." She grinned. "I see more lipstick. Just a minute." Brita pulled out the handkerchief again. "Keep your chin up." She licked a clean spot and dabbed it on the smudge that was by his ear. Brita couldn't help herself, but she prayed that he would kiss her again. "Done. You look much better. No one will know." She cleared her throat and felt herself getting hotter. She knew that she was probably the color of fire. "Now, I must check up on Ella," she said. She raised her arm and knocked once again.

"Okay," he said quietly.

Brita watched him leave, and told herself that keeping her distance was the right thing to do.

"Brita!" Ella exclaimed as she yanked open the door. "Your ears must be full of corn. That's why you didn't hear me tell you to come in here three times." She chuckled as she peered up and down the hallway. "Come on in!" Stepping aside, she let Brita enter. "What have you been up to?"

"I just wondered if you needed anything. Can I get you a glass of Ovaltine or chamomile tea?" Brita glanced around the room and noticed Ella's mysterious bag full of gadgets and noisemakers.

"Ovaltine? Tea?" Ella asked with a raised brow before shrugging. "Never touch the stuff. If I can't sleep, then I take a swig of blackberry brandy and that'll settle me right down. Haven't had to do that in ages. Thanks anyway, honeybun." She quickly slipped her nightcap on over her head. "I was just getting' myself set here. Anything else?" She put her hands in her robe pockets and waited for an answer.

"I'm curious—did you ever get that one sound figured out—the one you heard last night? Or was it the night before? We've been on this train too long… I'm starting to lose my sense of time. You didn't happen to see anyone come near my compartment, did you?" She thought of the knife and wondered if she should've said something to Ron about it.

"Have a seat, young lady. You look rather flushed." Ella motioned to the end of the bed. "Is it because of that fine young man that I saw strolling up the corridor? Good looking, too." She grinned. "Well… never mind, you don't have to answer. Now what was it you wanted again?"

"I'm just wondering about the night of the murder… that sound you heard, and if you saw anyone near my room," Brita said flatly. She wondered if it was noticeable to the world that she had a hankering for Ron? Brita frowned to herself for being so easily read.

"Nope. Never saw anyone near your compartment. Why?"

"Curious, that's all. What with Rose's compartment being so close to mine." Brita shrugged and felt a sense of danger returning. "What about the sound?"

"Sound?" Ella asked, puzzled, and then remembered. "Oh yeah. Just about got it." She reached for a piece of fabric that had one corner knotted and dropped it to the floor. "Hear that?" She did it again, and cocked her head. "It's real similar." She nodded to herself, smiling.

"I don't know what to say," Brita said. She took a moment to think. "What's tied in the end of it?" She reached for the fabric.

"A quarter, if that's what you're wondering." Ella said, and thrust the end into Brita's palm. "Feel that. See?"

"Interesting. Very interesting." Brita handed it back and kept her thoughts on Rose. "You heard that sound at the time that you were entering your room?"

"Yep. I'm positive. I glanced down at my feet because I thought I'd dropped something at the time. It was one of the rare times that this Silver Lady was threading across the plains."

"I'll keep this in mind," Brita said, deep in thought. "Well, since you're fine, I'll say good night."

"Okay. That was quick, but we're both tired. See ya later, alligator," Ella said, winking. "Don't let the bedbugs bite."

"I won't," Brita said, chuckling as she walked out the door.

Brita hesitated by her door, and wondered if she could go to sleep. It'd been a very long and exhausting day. She also wanted to jot down some ideas about Rose.

Pulling out her key, she slipped it in the keyhole and opened the door. The minute she stepped inside, she had a feeling as if someone had been in snooping. She shivered and ran her hands up and down her arms. It was just a passing fancy, she told herself, but let her eyes search the room. Nothing seemed to be out of place, except maybe her comb and brush set... but they could've moved from the vibrations of passing trains. The book beside the bed was slightly askew as well. She opened it up and shivered once again, feeling relieved. The gun was exactly where it should be, and the knife was definitely in her pocket.

It suddenly felt as if a cold north wind had swept through the compartment. She reached for the extra blanket and draped it around her shoulders, clutching the corners with white knuckles.

After a few moments, Brita opened her suitcase. Her clothes fell over the sides of the suitcase like feathers drifting in the wind, which made her raise her eyes and thank God that no one knew what kind of a mess she kept her things in. She should've known that there'd be no way that she could tell if anyone had searched, because she never folded her dirty laundry.

Brita removed her mystery book, notebook, pencil, and nightgown before shoving the suitcase aside. With a sigh of relief, she removed her suit coat before unzipping the skirt and letting it fall to her ankles. After settling her nightgown over her thin frame, she settled against a pile of pillows.

To take her mind off the knife, she thought of Rose. She went over and over everything that had been said between them, and what she'd heard in passing. Brita reached for her notebook and wrote down the names of the people that Rose had spoken to. They were mainly the folks from the Twin Cities Z; the Bakkos, Magnussons, Swensen, Jacques, Carlo, and Father O'Malley. She couldn't think of anyone else. Which of those people would have a reason to kill Rose, she wondered? There was one other person that had caught her attention, but he barely spoke to anyone. The man who dressed in the pinstripe suits and loud ties... George something. Was the killer still on the train? He could've returned the knife as a parting gesture, killed Rose, then left.

Rose was from the Twin Cities area; Brita thought maybe St. Paul. She'd have to ask Dwight when Rose had come onboard, just to be sure. It could have something to do with the murder. Then Brita thought about the newspaper and the section that it was opened to, and wondered if that was a clue? Brita wrote down St. Paul, newspaper, and Seattle streetcar token. She closed her notebook and set it aside.

Glancing out her window, she noticed the set of car lights driving away from the depot. The many stores with upstairs apartments had lights on in the windows. She watched as someone shut some off, making it dark. "Good night," she whispered softly. Brita pulled her blinds and reached up to turn on the overhead light.

Before she fell asleep, she placed the derringer under her pillow and the knife under the mattress. When she closed her eyes, she tried to imagine Ron's kisses as a peaceful feeling enveloped her.

A slamming car door woke her up, and Brita glanced at her watch before shutting the light off. It was midnight. Pulling the covers up over her head, Brita dreamed once again that Ron was kissing her — only this time, he was lying beside her.

*****

In the lounge, Ron had a few women who came by and winked. Then when Gladys strode through, she blew him a kiss.

"Aren't you the man about town," Gladys said, winking. She wore a huge grin as she hustled toward him. "If I were you, I'd take a gander in the mirror behind you." She cocked her head and chuckled as his eyes opened wide. "Turn around and look."

"Good grief." He tried to brush the lipstick stains off his collar and the makeup from his sleeves. "I'd better call it a day."

"You do that, hotcakes." Gladys chuckled and looked at her watch. "Ten o'clock. I'm going to bed, where we all should be right about now."

Ron picked up the rag and wiped the counters and closed the lounge for the evening.

When he'd finished wiping everything down, Ron headed for the door just as Stan appeared. Ron drew in a deep breath and hoped that Stan wouldn't notice his collar or ask any questions.

"Good night," Stan said as they passed each other.

"Good night."

Ron made it to his compartment, then began pacing the floor. An eerie feeling descended upon him, and he knew he wouldn't get any rest. Something was just not right, and he couldn't figure out what it was that nagged at him. He wasn't convinced that a hobo or anyone local murdered Rose, because Burlington was such a peaceful town. A local killer would murder a man, not a woman, and then take his money and run. It didn't seem to be the case, however, and that was what bothered Ron. He wondered if she'd been molested.

Ron was going to have to find out if the two previous murders were connected to Rose. His thoughts went back to the silver dollar episode with Ole. Ole was telling Ron something, but he couldn't figure out what it was. Ron glanced outside and paused as he watched the lights start to be extinguished in town. He yawned and stretched. He recalled his question of what had made the coroner suspect Rose was murdered… then within a few short minutes, Ole had flipped the silver dollar in the air. Ron relived the moment, playing it back and forth. A good agent wouldn't give such a blatant clue away unless he seemed to think that it was necessary. Ole was a good agent and did his job well, which led Ron to believe that the silver dollar was the key. If it'd been placed in Rose's pocket, it wouldn't have meant anything. There weren't any signs or suggestion of her being interfered with, so that meant that the killer must have chosen the place.

The only place on her body readily available and easily accessible was her mouth. A silver dollar must have been placed in her mouth. The killer had put it there for a reason—but what? He also wondered if the streetcar token was Rose's and if she'd just dropped it when she was attacked. No one heard any screaming, so that made Ron believe that she'd been attacked from behind.

He slipped out of his clothes and plunked into bed. As he tried to fall asleep, his thoughts churned around the murder… then with a blissful relief, they went to Brita. Her lips had tasted so sweet, and Ron wished for more. He was happy that he'd caught himself before more had happened because of the mess they were already entangled in. However, his imagination started to run wild with thoughts of lying beside her, feeling her skin pressed against his as he fell asleep.

Chapter Twelve

The killer carefully folded the red bandana over the top of his head and tied a square knot on the back of his neck, he then tucked in any loose hair. He didn't want the tainted dust on his skin or hair. He sat cross-legged on the floor. Next, he placed the five coffee cups from the kitchen right-side up in front of him before reaching for the thermos bottle.

As he slowly and methodically measured out the finely ground poisoned feed, he wondered how such a small amount of pale yellow dust from moldy haystock could kill so many head of cattle upon ingestion.

Omaha was the prime location for something of that nature to happen. In Chicago, there were too many people around, but Omaha wasn't as populated. He felt that his plan of infiltrating and dropping the poison into the elevator intake grate was safe.

After measuring the feed, he painstakingly poured it back into the thermos bottle. He knew how much to pour out into each of the bins. He looked around the room and wondered where a safe place would be to hide the thermos. Inside his small suitcase, he had a satchel that fit over his shoulder. He stuck the container inside it. It was a military bag he'd stolen from an American, and would work as a disguise.

Now that Rose was gone, no one would know that he was German.

As he washed his hands, face, and hair, he thought of his commander. The commander had left it up to him where to enter the United States, and he'd chosen Seattle. It was a smart move, because of the Japanese on the West Coast. The border patrol would be less likely to check his passport than they would have in New York City.

He shoved his hand in his pocket and removed his coins, looking for the Seattle streetcar token. He thumbed through each of the coins, but couldn't find it.

Suddenly it occurred to him that he'd used it as the weight in his tie when he killed Rose. While he hung up the satchel, he wondered if the token could lead the police back to him. But since there wasn't anything to tie him to Rose, he didn't give it any more thought.

The satchel had a heavy zipper on the outside, but the inside also had another one to lock the inside pocket. In that zipper, he placed a tiny thread that would be barely seen. If someone were to open it, he'd know.

After he'd hung the satchel on the hook, he set his suit coat over it for cover.

While dressing for bed, an old claustrophobic feeling began to invade the room. He drenched his face in water again, and dried himself with a towel. The feeling didn't leave him. He opened the blinds and stared out the window toward the river, hoping that it would help. Panic began to strike, and his heart beat hard and fast. He wondered what to do since it was the dead of night, and he couldn't just go running outside without calling attention to himself.

He tried to picture himself in the outdoors where there was no one around, but he was gasping for air. He wiped the sweat from his brow and lit a cigarette.

Slipping on his sportcoat, he stepped into the corridor and quickly went to the nearest vestibule. Standing with his nose against the crack, he breathed in the fresh air. After a few minutes, he continued to the lounge and removed a flask from his inside pocket while he sat down in the nearest chair and enjoyed being alone.

Chapter Thirteen

Day Four

Brita gradually opened her eyes and listened. She thought that the engine would be growling and moaning, and the engineer would be preparing to leave… but all she heard was passing traffic. Yawning, she swung her legs over the side of the bed and stretched. She slid the blinds back and took a gander outside. The distant water had ripples across it, and the riverbank trees swayed. Pedestrians wore hats that were clasped down as the other hand clutched their coats tighter.

"Brrr," she muttered and frowned. Her watch read six a.m. "Why does morning have to come so early?" she asked herself.

Brita reached out and turned on the tap water and found that it was already warm. She washed, brushed her teeth, and did a quick shampoo by hanging her head over the sink and pouring water from a glass onto her hair. It was the best that she could do, considering there weren't any bathtubs on the train. Fortunately, her hair had a natural wave. Brita didn't need to put her hair up into little pin curls with bobby pins pressed against her scalp and try to sleep. After combing her hair, she removed her nightgown. The garment slid like a feather around her well-shaped ankles. She stepped out of the circle and reached for her garter belt and silk stockings. The final touch was to set the knife into her waist pocket and the derringer back into the book.

When she looked in the mirror and started to apply powder and rouge, she thought of Ron. The bright red lipstick that she began applying made her think of his kiss, and her heart began to pound. She definitely wanted him to kiss her again, to hold her in his embrace—even though admitting it would mean defeat. She'd vowed to herself to never be caught in another treacherous relationship, and Ron certainly could be the next one in line.

A knock on the door interrupted her thoughts.

"Just a minute," she called, annoyed. She took a last look in the mirror, combed through her hair once more, and then opened the door. "Yes? Oh… Gladys."

"Just checking to see if you're up and at 'em. It's time. It seems that we have our work cut out for us. There's no food. Nope. Not unless you like oatmeal," she said, astounded. "Can you believe it? But that's that." She shook her head and plunked her hands on her hips. "I can't believe it myself. We're going to have to take turns going for walks to get a bit of fresh air." She stared at Brita. "You ready?"

"Yes, I am," Brita straightened her shoulders military style, and jutted out her chin. "Let's go!" She marched out the door in front of Gladys, letting her close it behind them.

"Well, I'll be… you're awfully bouncy today," Gladys said, cocking her head. "Sprightly, too."

As they neared the lounge car, several voices wafted down the corrido. Most of the lounge tables already had men circled around them when Brita entered. Three women dressed in wool sweaters and skirts were seated in a booth and talking. They looked over at Brita before resuming their chatter. Swensen and Jacques were busy rolling dice, and she noticed the empty beer bottles and glasses in front of them.

"Have you had breakfast?" Brita asked Gladys casually. She was starving.

"Honey, I nibbled on some cookies that two marines gave me yesterday a long time ago," Gladys said annoyingly. "The passengers are asking all kinds of questions; some are wondering if there's a killer onboard these wheels, while others are wondering if it's a government conspiracy. My, my, my." She shook her head and sighed. "I'm going up on the observation deck."

"Okay. I'm heading to the dining car." A passenger reached up and tugged on Brita's arm. "Yes?"

"Where's the food? When do we get rolling?" the man grouched. His punched-in nose, big ears, and scraggly beard gave him a bulldog look. "It's faster walking."

"There is a war on, you know. The troops get first dibs at the food supply." Brita tried to ease his misgivings.

Brita went to the dining car to help serve up fresh coffee and orange juice.

"Harold, let me help." Brita took the pitcher of water went up and down the aisle, filling empty glasses.

"I think next time I'll drive," a gentleman growled. He took a sip of the water. "Stale water." He shook his head. "I want coffee."

"Honey, don't be so cruel," his wife said, soothing him. "It could be worse, we could be stuck in Ohio where that awful bakery was." Her double chin as she shook her head and frowned.

"Sorry about all of this, but there's been one thing after another and none of it can be helped." Brita tried to give them a big smile, but understood why they were upset. She was too.

Brita finished pouring water and coffee and passing out day-old doughnuts. She brought the pot and pitcher back to Harold. "Is there anything else you'd like for me to do?"

"I can manage. Thanks."

"Any time." She looked up as Gladys entered the coach. "What do ya say if we start some kind of game or something with the kids?"

"It's an idea, but you need to go and eat first. I hear your gut grumbling." Gladys sucked in a deep breath. "It's only mid-morning and I'm pooped. You must be getting a headache from hunger."

When Ron walked into the car, Brita smiled at him. He warmed her heart and she silently wished that he'd rescue her from Gladys.

"You look spiffy today," Ron said to her. He flashed her a

grin. "You've never looked better." He turned to Gladys. "Have either of you two had breakfast?" He glanced from one to the other.

"I haven't." Brita had to resist from jumping up and down with glee.

"Since we'll be here for a while, let's go to town and eat. Are you ready, Brita?" For Gladys' benefit, he said, "I want to buy one of those delicious rolls that everyone seems to be swooning over." He winked at Brita.

"I'm set. Just let me grab my cape." To Gladys, Brita said, "When I come back, I'll take over for you." She smiled and turned to walk away.

"I'm going to line up Harold to take over the lounge. I'll meet you in the depot," Ron said with relish.

The cool autumn air that seeped through the vestibule doors took Brita's breath away. Walking with Ron, then stopping for breakfast and possibly visiting some of the town's quaint buildings, sounded appealing. Brita hadn't been quite as excited as this for ages.

As she was leaving her door, Ella was just stepping out from hers.

"Where's the fire?" Ella asked quickly. Her eyes opened wide like an owl and seemed to sparkle with amusement. "I'm going after some more of those doughnuts. Care to join me?" A feathered, bright pink hat crowned her head, and she wore a long gray woolen coat with large red buttons. A whistle tied to the end of a string hung from her wrist.

"What is the whistle for?" Brita asked, unable to keep her eyes from it.

"In case I get mugged," Ella exclaimed. "Now. Are you comin' or not?" She slammed her door shut and made sure that it was locked.

"I'm meeting the bartender, Ron. We're going for breakfast, I think... but thanks for the invitation. If we're here much longer, I'll go there with you. Okay?" Brita stepped around her.

"Okay. I'm on my own," Ella said with a grin. She walked

away, humming.

Brita went inside her compartment and reached for her Zephyrette long cape. Instead of wearing the uniform hat, she put a scarf on her head. She didn't want the cold wind to mess up her hair.

She walked briskly back through the length of the car and into the next. Passengers were coming and going.

"Hey you! When's this bucket of bolts going to start rolling again?" George asked, still wearing the pin-striped suit. He tightened his jaw and glared at her.

"Can't say. Don't know any more than you. All I know is that the food's going to be delivered and we'll be on the road soon after. How's that?" Brita plunked her hands on her hips and gave him a smile, even though she wanted to faint from the strong smell of booze.

"Fair enough." He tipped his fedora to her before walking away.

"Thank heavens for fresh air," she said under her breath as she stepped outside.

Ron stood by the depot door, and smiled at her as she approached. He looked so dashing, and his smile was pleasing. Brita found that she yearned for another one of his kisses, and willed it to happen.

"Shall we go for a bite to eat before taking a stroll?" Ron smiled down at her. "Let's go to Mel's Diner. Shall we give it a try?" He squeezed her hand.

"I'd love to," Brita replied quietly. She moved closer to him.

Ron wrapped her arm around his before leaning down and kissing her forehead softly. Brita felt warm all over and realized that her resolve to never have another affair was dissolving. Brita pulled her other arm through the cape armholes and clasped it tighter to fight the wind.

"Look at the library," she commented as they circled up Main street. "We must stop in there before we head back to the train. I love libraries."

"You do? Well, all right then. We'll stop on the way back."

He clutched her hand tight. "Did you sleep well last night?" Ron glanced down at her. When she raised her chin toward his, he leaned over and kissed her lips. "Tasty. One is not enough."

"I think that we need to hurry and get to the diner." Brita smiled.

"Didn't you like that stolen kiss?" Ron teased. He led her past the barber shop where the candy cane sign twirled and swirled. The resolution he'd made last night had already vaporized.

Brita squeezed his hand while he led her to the corner stop sign. The school bell chimed in the distance, and the sounds of small children laughing rang out.

"Morning recess," Brita murmured. It felt good to have him steer her down the street and take charge of where to go. Being an only child and living on military bases most of her life, she'd had to learn to fend for herself. It was a treat when someone took charge, yet made sure that she was happy at the same time. "Are we almost to the diner? I hear my stomach grumbling something fierce."

"Yep. It's on the next block," Ron said with a smile. "The drugstore reminds me of the apothecary in London." He nodded across the street to the building.

"I guess you're right," Brita said. "When were you in London?" Her curiosity was piqued.

"A few years ago," he answered, shrugging.

"I see the Mel's Diner sign up ahead," she said when he didn't say anything more. The less she knew of him, the easier it would be to walk away after the train reached Denver.

As Ron opened the door for her, the bell chimed. Fresh plain or powdered sugar doughnuts, plus an assortment of homemade pies filled the glass cases that ran across the back wall behind the counter. The smell of fresh baking rolls, beef roasts, and chickens in the oven for the lunch crowd almost made her faint.

"It smells soooo good in here. I think I should bring my pillow and spend the night. I'm going to order one of everything." Brita's mouth watered and her stomach growled.

"I'll order half, and you can have the other half," Ron mused.

They sat down in the nearest booth.

The bench seats were a dark shade of maroon, and the gray-topped booths sparkled from cleanliness. There were gathered, blue-checked gingham curtains across the length of the windows. Boxed white salt and pepper shakers with red lids were at the end of the booth, with napkins held between them.

The waitress brought over two glasses of water with the menus. When she came back after giving them a moment to look over the offerings, Ron gave her a quick order of bacon, eggs, toast, and coffee. Brita asked for the same thing, plus a piece of apple strudel.

When she was out of ear range, Ron turned back to Brita. "Did you find out anything significant about Rose? Was there anyone she regularly spoke with, or anyone she had a problem with while on the train?" Ron figured out the meaning behind Ole's tossing of the silver dollar.

"Ella told me something last night, but I don't know if it means anything." She waited while the waitress set down the coffee cups and walked away. Brita took a swallow before continuing. "She'd heard a thump when she was opening her door, at the same time Dwight came to help her. It could be when the killer entered Rose's room."

"What kind of thump? Explain this to me." Ron studied Brita closely.

"You know she does radio sounds, so she tinkered with it for a while. Finally, she took a piece of silky fabric and tied a coin in the end and dropped it to the floor."

*****

"How interesting," Ron said flatly. His heart pounded. If that sound meant anything at all—and his instincts told him that it did—but of course the other murders didn't involve coins. He just couldn't figure out a connection. He was going to have to keep Brita within his sight at all times… and preferably off the train as much as possible. Besides the possibility of something horrible happening, he was starting to believe that he was falling in love with her.

Fortunately the waitress brought their food, and Ron didn't have to say anything for a while. Eating gave him a chance to think and put his thoughts in order.

"You're awfully quiet all of a sudden." Brita watched him as she spread strawberry jelly on her toast and took a bite. "What I said, does it mean anything?"

"I'm not positive." Ron's brow furrowed. "I think it tells us how the Seattle token got on the floor. It must've fallen from his pocket while he was crouched behind the door, waiting for her." Ron hoped that his explanation would satisfy her curiosity.

"Could be." Brita cleaned her plate. "The strudel was delicious." She took a sip of coffee. "I don't know what to think, really. I can't see how Mindel and Rose would be connected, so I tend to think that they're not… but my instincts tell me that they are." She shoved the plate aside before drinking the last of her coffee.

"Enough talk of murder." Ron pushed his aside, and said, "Let's get out of here."

"Good idea."

Ron paid the bill, then pulled his collar up tight as they walked out of the diner.

"Brr…" She pulled up her collar as well. "You'd think that it was almost winter, wouldn't you?" She gave him a half grin.

"It *is* almost winter. Let's go to the library and have a look around. We'll take our time." He held her elbow as they waited to cross the street.

"What about Gladys?" She looked over at him. "You're worried, aren't you?"

"No. I'm just tired of all this stopping and starting and stalling because of murders, that's all." Ron took her hand in his and squeezed it tight as they walked. "Let's take another way and look at the other buildings." He steered her down a side street.

"Okay." Brita clutched her collar tighter.

As they walked, they looked at the many houses, and Brita thought of days gone by. There were houses that were reminiscent of the Civil War period. They stopped at a corner where there was a marker that read: "Site of Iowa's First Capitol Building."

"Look at that," Brita said with a grin. She realized that Ron wasn't listening at all, and was in fact deep in thought.

They kept walking.

"Ron? We're almost at the library steps, and you haven't said a word." Brita clutched his arm as they stopped across the street. "Look at the magnificent clock tower. Isn't it beautiful?"

"Huh? Oh, sorry." He gulped and looked at Brita.

The quaint old library building was impressive, with its Michigan red sandstone walls and dark slate roof. The many church bell towers blended into the skyline. Brass lighting fixtures near the entrance lent themselves to the days of horse-drawn carriages.

"I wish there was time to go inside."

"We need to head back to the train. Duty calls, unfortunately." He grimaced to himself. He enjoyed clutching Brita's petite, fine-boned hand, which fit like a glove inside of his.

"Yes. I suppose you're right. Gladys will probably chew me out." Brita said. "I have a question for you?"

"What's that?" Ron asked as he led her through the doors and out into the street. He steered them toward the depot doors.

"Has it occurred to you that the killer may have known Rose for another reason?"

"What are you saying?" Ron asked.

"I know about Charlot Fortier. Call it instinct, but I believe the killer is the same for all three murders. If that's correct, then

Rose may have had a secret life."
"Such as?"
"She may have been an informant."
"Then this person could still be onboard."
"Exactly," Brita said.

Chapter Fourteen

Before they entered the depot, Ron dropped his hand from hers. He felt Brita stiffen. Ron wondered how he'd be able to concentrate and keep his mind on the OSS job, and still keep abreast of her security.

"Thank you for the pleasant meal," Brita said sweetly.

"It was fun," Ron agreed.

The public-address system crackled and popped as they stepped through the doors.

All aboard! All passengers heading for Kansas City are to board on platform number five! All aboard! All passengers going to Dallas-Fort Worth, Texas, are to board on platform number twenty! All aboard!

Ron gave her a serious look. "How about meeting up later tonight?" He smiled to himself at her beauty, but worried for her safety.

"No, thank you. I've got plenty of work to do." Brita tried to keep to her resolve of never becoming involved again. "You do too."

"Please be careful," Ron said. "Truly, we don't know for sure how Rose died, or if the killer is still with us. Try not to talk much on the side, if you know what I mean."

"I do. I'll stick to business. If anything different catches my eye, I'll let you know."

They continued onto the train, where gruff voices rose and fell in cadence.

"I'm going to get started after I hang up my cape," Brita told him once inside the lounge car, then briskly walked away.

"Back to work." Ron went behind the counter.

The announcer spoke again, and instantly all noise from the bar room stopped. Older gentlemen cupped their ears, and women stared at the speakers.

This is Stan the conductor. I am happy to inform you that the Silver Lady will be departing from the beautiful town of Burlington in two hours. Our expected arrival time in Omaha, Nebraska, will be at seven in the evening. Please enjoy the ride, and I hope that you will travel again with Burlington Railroad. Over and out.

Brita quickly glanced over her shoulder to Ron, but he was too busy to look in her direction. With Gladys approaching, she didn't have the time to give the killer any more thought.

"It's about time that you returned. This place has been a complete zoo. I tell you, it's been awful. I haven't been able to turn around without someone giving me you-know-what kind of grief because we've been stuck here… as if it's my fault." Gladys plunked her hands on her hips and let out a long breath. "What'd ya have to eat?"

"Pancakes," Brita lied, because Gladys didn't need to know everything. "I'm going to hang up my cape and then head to the observation deck… or do you want me to go to another car?" Brita gave her a smile and waited, letting Gladys catch her breath.

"Sounds good, toots. I've circulated all the newspapers around, and brought enough cups of tea for a lifetime to the passengers. Now it's your turn. I'm going to the dining car where I don't have so much running to do. Land sakes, I wish I'd brought roller skates along."

In a flurry, Gladys was gone. Brita gave herself a moment to catch her breath. She noticed clouds still hovered in the distance when passing from one car to the next. Trees bent in the increasing wind. The library clock stood against the wind.

Brita opened her door and quickly stepped inside the room.

She hung up her cape and shed the scarf from around her neck. Once she'd folded it neatly and placed it inside her cape pocket, Brita raised her skirt and removed the knife. She placed it beside the derringer in the hollowed-out book. When she looked in the mirror, she decided to run the comb through her hair before reapplying lipstick.

Brita stepped into the hallway and noticed Dwight was seated in his spot and writing. She went over to him.

"We're finally going to get moving," she said.

"Yes, and not a moment too soon. There's been plenty of grumbling," he replied. "I'm going through the passenger list, and this car is full of people from Minneapolis. No one has bought tickets for Rose's room as of yet, but there's still time." Dwight looked up to her. "Does that answer all of your unasked questions?"

"Same folks?" Brita cocked her head. "I'd a thought that at least a couple would've left."

"They like the Zephyr." Dwight shrugged.

"I'm going up to the observation deck to work, in case anyone is looking for me."

"Okay." Dwight watched her walk away.

When Brita reached the top of the observation deck stairs, she stared out at the crossing gate tower. Through the tower's small windows, she watched the gatekeeper's shadow as he drew back the station sign with a rope to switch signs. The tower itself was so small that Brita wondered how anyone could stay inside of it for hours and hours, day after day, without becoming claustrophobic. Being a Zephyrette suddenly didn't seem like such a bad job. A baby cried, and Brita switched her thoughts to the present situation as she walked over to the women passengers.

"Do you think we'll leave any sooner than expected?" a mother asked, cradling her baby. "This is a hardship. I'm not sure if I'll travel on the Zephyr ever again." She smiled down at the baby, but then frowned at Brita.

"I don't know anything more than you do," Brita said

honestly. "All I know is that we're stalled because of the death and the food shortage, and it's not the fault of Burlington. Things just happen." Brita tried to sound pleasant, but she noticed that the women all seemed to sigh together, as if they'd resigned themselves to having an unpleasant ride.

"My husband is going to write a letter once I get home, and he'll let the railroad know exactly how poor the service has been," another woman huffed. Her baby began to cry, and the toddler beside her fell into her shoulder as a train whooshed past them.

"I don't know what to say," Brita conceded. Once more, she wished that she'd joined the WACS. "I'll talk to the conductor about it. Can I help you with anything?" When the women shook their heads, Brita walked toward the front of the deck.

The mothers occupied the u-shaped front observation seating, and had turned it into a child's playroom. There were at least twenty young women sitting and conversing, with ten children playing on the floor. Wood blocks were scattered, linen napkins were floating through the air like parachutes and one mother was teaching the older children how to construct dolls from the plants that had been in the dining car table vases.

"You women sure know what to do in times of trouble," Brita replied. "The children are so quiet and busy. I'm impressed." She smiled.

"Shush now! We don't want them to think they're being good, then they'll become naughty."

"Can I be of any service?" Brita asked. "I'll watch the children if anyone wants a break?" Brita glanced at each of the women.

"No, we're fine. However, once we start moving and it gets near supper time, then we might need help." The lady stacked the blocks for a child to push over.

"I'll make sure to come back," Brita said.

There were two gentlemen seated by a side window that she hadn't noticed. One had a beautiful white beard and sparkling eyes. The other was younger. He wore a black suit with a wide white tie, and a watch chain draped from his front pocket. He also stared out the window.

"Can I help either of you gentlemen?" Brita asked, leaning over the seat. "It's very inconvenient, isn't it? I'm truly sorry for the wait."

"No problem, ma'am," the young man said. "I'm looking out and thinking about nothing except my wife and kids waiting for me." He yawned, and then said, "Tonight, I'll be home."

"Good for you. I'm sure that your wife will be happy to see you." Brita smiled.

"Yes, ma'am." He thought for a second and asked, "Are there any current newspapers?"

"I'll look, but it's doubtful."

"Keep an eye out for me, too," the older gentleman said. He reached for a paper in the seat beside him. "Maybe I've missed something in here from the last read-through." He winked at Brita.

"You never know." Brita watched him hold up the paper.

"Hey. I did miss something. There's an article in here about decayed teeth causing heart attacks. Now that's news," he exclaimed.

"Really? Interesting," she said softly. "I'll come back to see how you two are doing soon."

During the next couple of hours, Brita walked up and down and back and forth, bringing tea and cookies to passengers, as well as newspapers. At one point, she watched two small children while the mother took a short nap.

Finally, the train began to roll slowly out of the yard. Brita watched out the windows as the late afternoon sun peeked through the clouds. With the train now traveling, it opened the view of the town for all to see. Clean streets and avenues stretched out of the town, amplifying the many picturesque, tall white houses. Oak and elm trees lined the paved streets and benches lined the curbs, offering up their welcome to the many visitors. The American flag waved in the wind as it hung in front of the store windows. Up the hill, the school loomed and Brita noticed a crowd of children outside playing. A large flag flew from the top of the pole. Down the street were the post office and courthouse, with each structure displaying a waving flag. The library was located on a different street, and also had a waving flag. The red, white, and blue gave her heart purpose.

Brita was thirsty, so she headed for the dining car. Her legs ached from all of the walking. The booths were full of people and there wasn't a spot for her to rest, so she went to the lounge. She sat down, and noticed that Ron hadn't taken his eyes away from her.

"I'd like a 7-up, please. I'm dying of thirst," she said with a smile. She let out a long sigh before yawning. "Sorry." A blush dotted her neck and trailed down into her décolletage.

"Here you are," Ron whispered. "I'm going to die," he muttered under his breath. He knelt down for a rag.

"You're not sick, are you?" she asked between swallows. "You look pale." She raised a brow when he shook his head.

"Just thinking," he answered lamely, busying himself wiping the counter.

"Thanks." Brita set down the empty bottle and walked away.

"You're welcome," Ron said, cracking his fingers.

As Brita reached the top of the stairs, the speaker buzzed.

This is your conductor, Stan, speaking to you again. The Silver Lady is once again rolling across the prairie. The dining car is open and will be serving dinner. Please enjoy your ride. Thank you for riding Burlington. Over and out.

Ron kept himself busy pouring drinks for the passengers. Stan had stopped by and told him to offer free drinks to the regular customers as a way of saying thanks, and said that they'd stick to the usual hours, so the lounge would close by eleven.

Ron was beginning to think that the itch he felt for Brita was worth the chance. The manner in which each different woman walked and held her head, even the bounce in her steps reminded him of Brita. Now he was seeing her in other people… he even smelled her perfume on every woman. It was beginning to make him wonder about his sanity.

"Is your daydream pretty?" Swensen asked with a leer as he set his empty beer bottle down.

"What? Oh! Sorry, I was just thinking," Ron replied hurriedly. He took the empty bottle and replaced it with a new one.

"So the train's rolling again. Good. It's about time," Swensen said. He took a few swallows, planting his rearend on the barstool. He rested his arm on the countertop. "Any news?"

"No, not really. I'm just happy to be going again, that's all," Ron said, stifling a yawn. "Why aren't you rolling dice?"

"Jacques is busy chasing some dame." Swensen shrugged. He turned and looked toward the poker table. "Looks like there's room for one more." He took his bottle and walked away.

As Ron watched him go, another customer came forward.

"Father O'Malley, what would you like?"

"I'd like a brandy water, please. 'Bout time this thing gets rolling." He tugged on his collar and wiped his brow. "It's hot in here." He handed Ron the money.

"Nope. On the house." Ron brushed the priest's payment away.

Ron had trouble keeping focused on his job because all that went around in his head was Brita. He imagined undressing her.

He found that he was wiping his brow more than usual.

George came over and placed a newspaper down on the counter, interrupting Ron's thoughts.

"It's great to be moving, ain't it? What can I get you?" Ron asked, giving him a smile. He'd noticed more than once that George always made people chuckle, but rarely smiled himself. Ron had been watching him ever since they'd left Chicago, and found him curious.

"It's about time we're on our way again. I'd like a whiskey with a beer chaser. And an available dame… any kind will do."

"Here you go." Ron chuckled and placed the full shot of whiskey in front of him. George drank it right down.

"Another," George ordered. He shot it back as well, then grabbed the bottle of beer. "Thanks," he called over his shoulder.

"Anytime." Ron shook his head as he watched George go to the poker table.

He looked up and saw Gladys entering the lounge.

"Thirsty?" he asked. Ron held up a bottle of grape Nehi as Gladys approached, and opened it when she sat on a stool.

"Thanks." She took a few quick swallows, then wiped her mouth. "Right on the mark."

"It's going to be a long night, I fear," Ron said, trying to make himself sound nonchalant. "What time do you think we'll be able to go to bed? I'm kind of tired."

"Honey, you're crazy if you think that you can close up the bar now. It's only four o'clock. I rarely get to see my bed before ten every night, if I'm lucky to have someone helping." She arched her brow before drinking the soda. "Mighty good tasting, and it hit the spot." She covered her mouth as she burped. "Excuse me. Now I must get going."

She muttered under her breath as she walked away. "Tired? He should walk a mile in my shoes… standing behind a bar all day… he doesn't know what tired is."

Ron watched her shaking her head as she walked away. A woman's voice calling for a bartender caused him to look in the other direction.

"Ella! Whatcha need?" He gave her a smile.

"I think you can help me out a bit. I'm dying of thirst, but I also want to steal some of those pop bottle caps, if you'd be so kind." She chuckled, then arched a brow.

"Certainly. Whatcha drinkin'?" Ron asked, amused.

"7-up."

"You trying to make more sounds from these things?" He

reached into the container and pulled out ten caps.

"Crickets, actually," she answered, taking the caps and dropping them into a little square box that fit into her knitting bag. "Thanks a bunch."

"Here," Ron said, handing the bottle to her. "It's on the house. You're in the room right down from Brita, aren't you?" He gave her a smile.

"Yep, sure am. I've got a few sounds all figured out that I thought I'd try out on her." Ella picked up the bottle. "She's coming to my room later, and it'll take a while. I have to get these perfected before I do my next radio show." She hobbled away, the bottle in one hand and knitting bag in the other.

Chapter Fifteen

Voices rose and fell; some sounded angry, others pleasant as Brita entered the dining car in search of an ice bag. A child had fallen and now had a big goose-egg on his forehead. Brita had to hurry before it got worse. The mother was frantic.

The steady rocking of the train made walking slightly treacherous. Once Brita reached the dining car Harold gave her ice and cookies for the little boy. The cookies were stuffed into her pocket so that she could clutch the ice bag in one hand and hang onto the railing with the other.

As Brita entered the lounge car, she noticed a man's back arch stiffly, and he suddenly rolled off the seat. He landed with a thud onto the floor. A woman screamed. Brita dropped the ice bag and raced over toward him.

"Stand back! He's having an epileptic seizure." she ordered. "Move back… give him space. He needs air! Ron!" Brita watched as the man's legs kicked and twitched, while his eyes rolled back and his head rocked from side to side. "Open up the floor space… give him room! He needs air!" She looked toward the bar and noticed that Ron wasn't there. "Ron! Someone give me a spoon!" A passenger handed one over, and Brita carefully inserted it into the man's mouth to prevent him from choking on his tongue. "This only lasts a few minutes. He'll be fine." Brita tried to calm everybody down. The women had covered their mouths in shock, and the men stared. She looked toward Ron's direction just as he parted the crowd of people and pushed his way through to her.

"What in the world?" Ron asked, leaning over Brita. "What is this? I've never witnessed anything like this before."

"Epileptic seizure. He'll be fine, but very tired. He needs a quiet place to rest. Look. He's starting to calm down," Brita said.

She remembered that Rose's cabin was currently being used for storage, as no one wanted to sleep there. "Let's put him in Rose's compartment. No one will bother him, and the doctor can examine him in private there."

"I'll go and get Dwight. We'll be back shortly. It won't take long to move out the food boxes and baggage that we'd stored in there." Ron stood up, and quickly walked away.

Just as Brita was taking the man's pulse, Gladys came over, wrecking her concentration.

"Did someone die again? Someone died, I just know it. Who is it now? There you are, right in the thick of things… again. Good Lord, Brita, can't you stay away from dead people? They swarm around you like flies!" Gladys leaned over and sniffed. "He don't smell of death. He ain't dead, is he?"

Brita stood up and stepped back.

"I was just trying to take his pulse when you interrupted me. It's all under control. Mr. Healy and Dwight will carry him to Rose's room, where Dr. Feinstein can have a look at him." Brita took in a deep breath, was happy to see that most of the passengers had sense enough to get back to whatever it was they were doing.

"Can I help?" Gladys stayed far back.

"Yes. There's a little boy on the observation deck who fell and hit his head. I was taking him an ice bag, but then this happened. The bag is right over there." Brita indicated where it was by nodding. "Will you see to him? I'd give you the cookies that I was going to bring him, but they're all crunched up." Brita prayed silently that Gladys would leave.

"Sure. The poor little guy. Bet he has a terrible goose egg, too. Poor thing." She shuddered before reaching over for the bag.

Brita was relieved when Gladys left the area. She went back to taking the man's pulse. It was slightly erratic, but there didn't seem to be any cause for concern. She'd tell the doctor what it was when she saw him.

The man's eyes were starting to focus by the time that Ron and Dwight entered the lounge.

"We can take over from here," Ron said as the two of them lifted the man to his feet and helped him walk to Rose's room.

Brita followed, opening and closing the vestibule doors. Once they reached the compartment, they helped him lie down on the bed.

"Dwight, please get the doctor. I'll stay to monitor him."

"I have to get back to work, Ron told Brita. Keep me posted.".

She closed the door after her two helpers.

Brita gently removed the man's shoes, untied his tie, and loosened the top shirt buttons, then covered him so that he'd stay warm. It didn't take long before Dr. Feinstein entered the room.

"His name is Mr. Lovejoy," she told him. "I just looked in his wallet."

"Good." Dr. Feinstein replied. "You put the wallet back, I trust?"

"Of course," Brita fumed. "I wouldn't steal. I'm a Zephyrette, as well as a general's daughter."

The doctor studied her for a minute before beginning his examination. It seemed like hours, but at last the doctor said that she could leave as long as they both kept a close eye on him. All he needed was sleep. Brita was relieved, because being in the room made her feel queasy and uncomfortable. She needed to get out before she became sick, as it brought back too many unhappy memories.

"I'll be in the dining car for a while, but I will check on him when I'm through." Brita excused herself and walked out.

*****

The killer had found the right moment to replace Brita's underwear. He'd kept it until the train was moving. Now he could taunt and bait her. Killing the general's daughter would add to his list of heroic acts, and might lead to a promotion.

Taking a virgin would be his ultimate prize.

As the man had been ministered to in the lounge, he'd sneaked out of the car and headed for his room. After he'd dropped a couple kernels of untainted corn into his pocket, he'd sneaked toward her room and slipped inside.

At first he couldn't locate the book, but eventually found it in her suitcase. Next to the knife, he placed the corn. After he put the book back and closed up the suitcase, he stuck her panties under her pillow.

"The game's afoot."

He crept back to his compartment, laughing softly.

*****

Ron finished serving drinks to two couples before going into the dining car. It was full of people, but he found a table in the back corner. He hoped that Brita would surprise him.

As he waited for Harold to give him the menu, he opened the newspaper George had left on the bar. Several stories caught his interest. There was a story about grain rust being found in the fields of Germany. Another story was about police clamping down on Nazi sympathizers. Ron looked up when Harold set the menu down.

"The special is a ham dinner. Iowa ham is the best in the country, I might add. Otherwise, take a gander at the menu," Harold said. "Coffee?"

"Yes, and the special." Ron handed him back the menu.

"Ham dinner, coming right up."

He glanced up to see Brita entering the room, and waved to her. She joined him.

"This is a great spot." She slid into the booth. "Have you ordered?"

"Yes. How are you? I bet you're starved." He kept his gaze glued to her, and thought about how beautiful she was.

"How did you know that I'm starving? I'm very tired, too."

"Have you ever treated someone with epilepsy before? I feel

sorry for him." He gave a quick smile.

"Mr. Lovejoy will be fine. He just needs sleep. I'll check in on him later," Brita said, and shivered She looked down at the table.

Harold brought over Ron's coffee and set it down with his plate. "Enjoy." He turned to Brita. "I bet you'd like the same?"

"Yes, please." She leaned back in her seat and gazed into Ron's eyes. She looked away quickly, suddenly shy.

"Here, take my plate. You deserve it. I'll wait." He pushed it in front of her. "Go ahead."

"Thank you," she said softly. "They're watching us." She nodded toward them.

"We're just eating. There's nothing wrong with that," Ron said. "I like being with you."

"You too," Brita said with a lump in her throat.

"Your plate, Ron," Harold said, coughing. "Enjoy." He nudged Ron's arm.

Brita ate silently, barely tasting the food. She was certain that it was delicious. The ham smelled like Easter Sunday, the carrots and peas were delicious, and the potatoes were fresh picked and straight from the field.

"I'm glad that we finally were able to get rolling and out of Burlington," Ron said, just to make conversation. He cleaned his plate.

"Yes." Harold set down a fresh cup of coffee for her, and she said, "Thank you." drank it.

Ron cleared his throat. "It was very good. But I really should get back to work."

"Me, too. I have Mr. Lovejoy to check on, and I think Ella wants to try out a few sounds on me." Brita finished her last bite and drank down the coffee. "Yummy."

"I agree." Ron stood and held out his hand to her.

"Thank you." When Brita placed her hand in his, she felt a tingle all the way up her arm.

Together, they walked away. The train seemed to do a little jump on the tracks, catching Brita by surprise. Ron reached out and clutched her arm before she fell.

"Thanks." Her heart skipped from his touch. She presumed that Ron went behind the counter as she walked away.

Stan's voice popped onto the overhead speaker, and Ron watched as most people cupped their ears to listen, either setting down their cards or just plain shutting up.

This is Stan, the conductor. We will soon be entering the beautiful town of Council Bluffs, Iowa and then we'll be stopping overnight in Omaha, Nebraska for loading supplies. I hope that you've enjoyed your ride on the Burlington Zephyr. It is nine o'clock. Have a good night. Over and out.

Ron continued serving drinks, but his thoughts were on Brita. He pictured her as she ate. The image of her tasty mouth went through his mind, as did her blush, which went down the length of her shapely neck. He'd tried to shrug it off, because he really didn't want his fingers broken, but couldn't.

He vaguely remembered Swensen paying for a couple of beers, as well as Father O'Malley and George, the latest barstool sitter. Most of the customers kept to themselves. When he next looked at his watch, it was nearing ten-thirty. Ron went over to wipe down the tables and booths as the room became empty.

As he noted that the employees were beginning to return to their stations, Ron drew in a deep breath.

Brita would be checking up on Mr. Lovejoy and then go to Ella's room.

Ron closed up the bar and headed down the many long corridors and through the several vestibules until reaching the passenger coach car. His eyes opened wide when he found Brita talking with Stan.

"Mr. Lovejoy woke. Dwight helped him to his compartment, where he'll stay for the rest of the night. He's very tired, but in fine condition," Brita said.

"Good. At least it wasn't too serious," Stan replied.

"How is Ella this evening?" Ron asked nonchalantly. He

stood beside them so Stan couldn't see his face.

"I've already been to see her. I was going to make one last round of the passengers before going to bed," she answered with a smile.

"Remember," Stan said, looking from one to the other. "You both have work to do. Stay professional." He studied each of them before leaving.

"Yes, sir. I understand," Brita muttered. "I'm going to finish my duties, then go to bed. Good night."

She walked away before Ron had a chance to say anything.

Ron noticed that her shoulders were slightly slumped and her steps weren't as brisk as they usually were. It was as if she'd been deflated. Ron stayed behind Stan as he walked into the sleeping car.

The train gradually slowed as they got closer to Omaha. Ron found it harder to keep his footing. Staying behind a bar or only walking a little bit while it moved had its advantages.

Ron decided to step into the men's bathroom, which was right inside of the sleeping car and across from Rose's room. It would give him the advantage of knowing who was coming or going. That was his immediate plan.

Someone was in the bathroom, and the door was locked. Ron waited in the vestibule, nodding to passing passengers. When the man stepped out, Ron slipped inside and locked it. Whenever someone walked past, he'd unlock the door and peer out. As the train began to slow down, a man crashed into the door and it popped open.

"Thanks. I've been stuck inside of there for a long time. You saved my life." Ron figured a going with a little white lie was smarter than telling the truth.

The train jiggled and the brakes swooshed, then finally it was silent except for the drone of the engines.

Ron opened his door and left it open, deciding to pretend that he'd forgotten to shut it. He sat on his bed and watched as people came and went, but didn't see Brita. She could come in from the other direction so he wouldn't see her, but he would hear when she opened her door. That was what he was waiting for. Once she'd gone to her compartment, he wondered how he'd be able to enter it? It'd be almost impossible to invite her into his, with all the people roaming about. Then it occurred to him… a costume was in order.

As Ron shut his door, he rubbed his hand down his scruffy chin. He shaved so that his face was smooth when he wore his costume.

He opened his suitcase and pulled out all of his clothes. Tucked in the back corner and under layers of underwear, he found what he was looking for, an old garment he'd worn as a disguise when he was in the French Resistance. Removing his shirt, pants and shoes, he thought about how silly the whole thing was and almost quit, but then he remembered how tasty Brita was and how much he wanted to kiss her again.

Fortunately for him, his mother had had several children, so her figure had changed over the years. The dress almost fit him around the waist. Ron sucked in his breath as he buttoned it. He folded up handkerchiefs and stuck them in the heels of his shoes to give them a slight high-heel look. He looked in the mirror as he tied the scarf on his head and put the shawl over his shoulders, and thought of a Russian peasant woman.

He heard Brita humming and putting her key in the door. He quickly put on the gloves and set out of his room to knock on her door.

"Hurry up," he muttered. Ron held his breath as a passenger came down the corridor, and he didn't let it out until he'd gone by. He knocked again. The door across the way opened and closed.

"Just a minute," Brita answered. She applied fresh lipstick and combed her hair.

"Brita?" he said when she opened the door.

Brita looked into his eyes and chuckled, swinging the door wide open. Ron slipped in, shutting it behind him.

"What in the world?" she asked, laughing. "Why? Whose dress is it? Is there something that you're not telling me?" She collapsed on the bed.

"It's my mother's." He pulled her up into his arms and held her close. "You smell wonderful."

"This isn't right. We can get into trouble. Remember, we have to stay professional." She tried to keep up her strength against him.

"No one will ever know," he whispered. He placed tiny kisses on her ear and neck. When she sucked in her breath, he searched for her mouth as she shivered from his touch. "Please?"

"Kiss me," she breathed. She kissed him closing her eyes, she wrapped her arms around, growing warm with every kiss.

Brita's heart tripped as he encircled her in his arms and ran his hands up and down her back. He placed hot kisses along her neck and up to her ear, whispering how pretty she was. Gradually, his palms smoothed over her sides and came around to her face, holding her as he stared into her eyes.

"You taste so good." Ron kissed her again.

"Well... grandma..." Giggling, Brita brought her hands up to his head and pulled the scarf off. Wrapping her arms around him, she kissed his neck and chin and lips, nuzzling into the crook of his neck and sighing with joy. She felt as if she might burst when he started kissing her hard on the lips.

Brita's breath caught in her throat as his strong hands traveled up and down her sides—then realized what she was doing.

"Are you sure?" He gave her delicious kisses on her neck and ear.

"We'd better quit." She had trouble believing that she'd said it. "We can't... it's not right." Brita knew they had to stop.

"You're right," Ron said, still holding her in his arms. "I'm sorry. It's just that... well... you taste so good, and you're so beautiful." When she looked up at him, he kissed her lightly. "I'll go."

"Right." Brita clung to him.

"I'd better leave right now." He kept his arms around her.

"Right now." When she nodded, he slipped his arms down and backed up.

"I'm so sorry." She fought back tears.

"Honey, don't be. I'm a brute." Ron reached for his scarf and placed it on his head.

"Let me tie it," she murmured. With shaky fingers, she tied the scarf under his chin, then stepped back and giggled. "You'll fool everyone."

"Thanks. Good night," he said, staring into her eyes. He hated to leave.

Brita went to the door and cracked it open before looking out. "It's clear."

After she'd closed the door, tears welled in her eyes and she sighed.

Chapter Sixteen

Day Five

The killer stayed awake and watched the railyard men come and go. The bull was easily detected, because he stood with watch in hand and scribbled down when someone came and went from the back towers. He also swung the lantern with authority as he walked.

He wasn't quite sure where the stockyards were located in relation to his position. The deep thunder of the cattle was distant, but still made his heart pound.

He slipped his cigarettes into his shirt pocket, then put his Swiss army knife in his overcoat pocket. His gun went under his shoulder, and he strapped another knife on his ankle. He opened his bag, placing his few belongings inside with the thermos of contaminated cattle feed. He placed it over his shoulder and found his flashlight and hat before opening the door and slipping out.

As he headed toward the vestibule a tall, husky peasant woman stumbled into him.

*****

Brita leaned into the closed door, shutting her eyes. Tracing her fingertips from her lips to her breasts, her breath came in shallow spurts as she relived his embrace, touch, and kisses. When she licked her lips, it seemed as if he were still kissing her. Her body ached for more.

As Brita removed her uniform coat, she let out a long sigh. The skirt dropped around her ankles and she scooped it up. While she hung them up, Brita imagined what it would be like if Ron had removed them. She rolled down her silk stockings and unhooked her garter belt, dreaming that someday soon, Ron would be helping her to undress. She noticed her pants and sweater had fallen to the floor. She was cold and decided to wear them until she warmed. An odd feeling overcame her and she opened her book, her panties were beside the knife. She removed the knife and double-shot derringer, loaded it and flipped on the safety latch.

"That monster..." she murmured. The horrible memory replayed in her mind. With her heart pounding, she glanced out the window and saw shadows and movement.

Moving closer to the window, she studied the figure of a man passing by. She pushed into the pane and watched as her eyes grew wider with fear.

She asked herself if it was him as she stayed glued to the spot. She had to wipe the window clear from the steam of her panicked breath.

Fear seized her and her heart raced. It felt like time stood still as the memories flooded back; his walk, the way the overcoat draped, that hat. It all reminded her of Mindel's killer. She was positive. She glanced away and then looked back, studying his gait. It was him, and he was getting away!

Guilt flooded through her, and Brita bit back the tears. The bastard wasn't going to escape again. She'd bring him to justice. She quickly slipped on her walking shoes and parka, but kept her eyes on the killer so she could keep track of his movements.

"It's payback time," she whispered and opened the knife.

She glanced out the window and watched as the figure began to slip out of view.

Closing the knife in one quick stroke, she dropped it into her parka pocket. She grabbed the derringer and slid into her pants pocket. In the other pocket, she dropped additional bullets.

Brita set out and crept down the corridor as fast as she could. After entering the first vestibule, she tried the door; it was locked, as were all the others that she tried. That meant that the killer didn't plan to return, which made Brita glad she hadn't wasted time telling Ron.

Continuing toward the lounge car, she found it unlocked. She slipped out into the cold, blustery prairie wind.

Brita stood for a moment to figure out where she'd last seen him. Unlike last time, she wasn't going to stumble.

Keeping behind the cars and out of the yard light shadows, she made a dash to catch up with a killer.

*****

Ron paused as he made his way back to his room after bumping into a man in the corridor… something nagged at him. He took two more steps, stopped, then turned around with a puzzled look on his face.

As he studied the man's retreating back, he came to the realization that his shoulder had bumped into a holstered gun.

Ron went to his room and slipped his shoes off. He stood up and unbuttoned the dress while his thoughts churned round and round over what had just happened. Instinct told him that something was wrong, but he couldn't put his finger on it. The weather didn't demand a heavy overcoat, not to mention the satchel over the man's shoulder and the concealed gun holster.

The description that Brita had given him about Mindel's killer came to mind, and the man from the hallway fit it. Ron shook the dress from his shoulders and stepped out of it, flinging it on top of the bed.

He saw a shadow thread a path under the yard lights through his window, and watched as the figure ran away from the railyard bulls. It was clear to Ron that he didn't want to be seen. Quite unexpectedly, he noticed a flash of blonde hair following him. It took him about two seconds to realize that it was Brita.

In a panic, he bolted out the door.

*****

Brita wasn't clear where the stockyards were located, but

she heard the distant rumbling of the cattle. The stench wasn't nearly as bad as in Chicago, so it made her believe that the stockyard was located at the Union Station.

The moon shone bright, and the Milky Way brightened the skyline, which helped Brita adjust to her surroundings. She was glad that she'd put on her walking shoes and pulled the hood over her head. While it wasn't unbearably cold, it was still the end of October, and winter was right around the corner. She stopped suddenly and her heart raced from a glimpse of a distant shadow.

The figure stopped for a smoke. Brita watched him look at something in his palm until he crushed the cigarette out with his shoe heel. All at once, he pivoted and went in a different direction, disappearing from sight.

The moonbeams shone across the flat layout of the Omaha yards. The floodlights spilled into the yards, exposing the separation of the tracks and cattle feedlots.

She hesitated. As she halted, she slowly became aware of the sound of crunching gravel coming from behind her.

Her thoughts spun as she wondered how he had he circled around her so fast. She tried to find her derringer as her eyes searched frantically for a hiding place. She ducked between two cars, her heart beating so wildly that she was certain it would give her away.

She clutched her gun in trembling hands.

*****

Ron stopped and looked where he'd last seen Brita. As he darted from one car to the next, his heart pounded. She could get killed, he thought over and over. The planes from the nearby military base couldn't drive out the fear that raced through his veins. Still he couldn't find her as he wove a path around the cars. Just when he was about to give up and circle back to the starting point, he saw a flicker of that moonbeam-drenched hair bob behind a car. Relief captured his heart as he moved quietly toward her. Just as he leaned over and was about to touch her arm, she spun around and pulled the trigger.

"Doggone it!" Brita's eyes opened wide, and she shoved him, hitting him hard in his chest, but happy to see him. "How dare you sneak up on me like that! If not for the safety, you'd be dead!"

"Ouch!" Ron had fallen on his backside from the unexpected blow. "Why are you here? Go back to the train right now," he whispered once he'd regained his composure.

"Why am *I* here? *You* go back to the train," Brita said.

"Tell me why you're here," Ron insisted. Clamping his palm on her shoulder, he forced her to stare into his eyes. "I need to know, and I need to know now."

"I saw the bastard who murdered Mindel. I'm positive it's him. He's been taunting me… in fact, he broke into my room and placed my knife back in my secret spot before we reached Burlington," Brita crossed her arms and glared at him. "And as if that's not enough…" Brita stopped. "Well, let's just say I aim to give him his due."

"Oh my God… Shit," he muttered under his breath. "What else? You're not telling me everything… What is it?" He stared at her.

"This was with it." Brita reached into her pocket and pulled out the picture. "I can't believe that Charlot is dead. He was such a good friend of my dad's." She kept her gaze on Ron. "What are you thinking?"

"I've heard of him…" he said under his breath. "I don't understand why he's here in Omaha. For some reason, he must be going to the stockyards." He took a deep breath. "Charlot wasn't in the picture that Sergeant Poloski found on Mindel's body, was he?" Brita shook her head. "Listen, just shut up and follow me—and don't, under any circumstances, go in front of me. Stay at my heels." He stared at her. "I mean it."

"That's what you think. You're just a bartender… at least I have some military training. You're following me." She gave him a look that would curl hair, then motioned which way she wanted them to go. "Follow me. It's payback time."

Soon they were alongside the Burlington depot. Ron held his arm out to prevent Brita from standing out in the open. She shifted to move abreast of him and stared into the street.

"Wait here." She held her hand up like a stop sign. Brita felt his glare all the way to her toes, but didn't care. She was not going to feel guilty because she let the killer slip through her fingers again.

Silently, she traced a path into the street before standing next to a street lamp. She scanned the nearby neighborhood and wondered if her target had decided to take a shortcut through the back yards. The wind blew the smell of the stockyards in their direction, and it almost made her stomach turn inside out.

Ron stared off into the direction of the stockyards. He scanned the treetops for silhouettes of little towers, the switching stations. The tower man raised or lowered the intersection stop signs as a means for traffic control. Ron spotted several in the distance, and motioned for Brita to come back as he slowly started to build a likely plan of the killer's mission.

"I think he's taking shortcuts through those back yards," she whispered. "I'm sure I saw him. Let's go."

"We should follow the tracks," he responded, annoyed. "Then we'll meet him at the stockyard and be ready. I think that's where he's heading. We could easily lose sight of him going through people's yards."

"I'm following my hunches." Brita glared at him. "Either you're with me or you're not. Which is it?" she asked, determined.

"Why are you so confounded stubborn? This is ridiculous. We're following a killer, assuming that you're right. You should be following me," Ron said, returning her glare.

"I know it's the same one who murdered Mindel. I will not let him get away again." She clamped her jaw and stared at him with fire in her eyes before turning and leaving.

"I can't believe I'm following you," Ron answered. He had

trouble keeping his mind focused as he followed her.

Their path gave them a workout as they cut through yards and went over picket fences.

Ron grabbed Brita's arm and pulled her behind a large tree. They stood for a few minutes until the dogs quit barking.

"I don't see him, and haven't for quite a while," Ron whispered. "I'm impressed with your conviction, but let's go to the tracks. At least that way we won't get lost." He noticed fire returning to her eyes.

"I saw him go this way, and this is the way that I'm going. You can go any way that you'd like." Brita was about ready to spit from frustration. She didn't want to admit that he might be right. She did feel lost. Plus, the excitement she felt when she was with Ron was almost dizzying at times. He was keeping such close watch on her, making sure that she didn't hurt herself—like when they leaped over the fences. Her heart fluttered when he touched her.

"Okay, have it your way," he said, defensively. "But this street runs parallel with the tracks. Let's just go and take a quick look, and maybe we'll see him." Ron wanted to kiss her. Her hair shimmered in the night like a lovely flower, and she smelled like a rose. His heart pounded.

"Oh, all right," she conceded.

They fled up the street and headed toward the nearest train track. Ron grabbed her hand as they set out to run across. Just as they approached it, the man inside the tower put the arm down to signal a train. The sign clinked and lights blinked.

"Stop!" the man shouted from inside of the tower. "Don't! You'll get hit!"

They stopped just as the train whooshed right beside them, taking their breath away. Ron pulled her into his chest. She thought for sure that she'd be lifted into the air as it sped by, but he kept her safe and warm. Her heart fluttered when he brushed his lips against her cheek before releasing her.

It wasn't until it had passed that she realized that she'd held her breath the whole time. Ron grabbed her hand again, and off they ran while the man in the tower cursed loudly at them.

Ron was sure that the killer had gotten away. He decided he had to trust in luck and good fortune to guide him.

Another train passed them, but they were on the correct side of the tracks. They stopped for a moment to catch their breath. Ron figured that they were alone, and it would be safe to speak.

"Where is he? The stockyard smell is getting worse." Her heart pounded. His tight grip on her hand was moist and spoke of fear.

"That's where he seems to be heading, and the man who bumped me in the hallway was carrying a satchel…" He knew by her actions that she would be willing to follow his train of thought.

"None of this makes any sense to me." She tugged his arm to get him to stop. "Do you agree that this person has killed all three victims?"

"Yes. Now let's get moving." He took her hand and they set off again.

The closer they came to the stockyards, the louder the thunder from the animals' movements seemed to rumble the ground under their feet. Trains were coming and going from the opposite side.

As they came to another intersection, Ron thought he saw him. He grabbed Brita's arm and they sank down behind a large bush to wait. They watched as he sat on a bench, lit a cigarette, and smoked it.

"My God, it's Swensen," Ron said softly. "What the hell is he doing?"

"I can't believe it," she replied, stifling a sneeze.

A dog barked when Swensen got up to move again.

"You're right. It's the drunk." Brita seethed as Ron squeezed her hand and waited a few minutes before following. They stayed behind him and gave him plenty of space.

*****

Swensen, also known as Captain Arnwolf, decided to

backtrack to check for tails. He circled back and waited behind a park bench and watched as two people slowly walked by. When they didn't appear to be looking at anything but one another, he started for the feed elevator again. He wanted to hide the cumbersome bag, but at the last minute changed his mind.

At last he came to the yards and stopped next to the massive Exchange Building, letting the building's shadow blanket him in darkness. It gave him a few minutes to watch and listen, and try to see the guard stations.

There were two men dressed in striped railroad overalls talking casually as they walked the perimeter. The police station was just ahead. Policemen continually patrolled that side of the yards. The captain chuckled to see guards around the stockyards, but none covering the elevators.

He scratched his head and leaned against the building. Off in the near distance, he noticed a slow-moving train, the brakes squeaking and squealing to move the first grain car into position for the grain inlet chute.

Reaching for another cigarette, he heard the faint sound of voices and quickly moved toward the front of the building. The tall archway allowed him the room to study the surroundings from a better vantage point. At last he was able to figure out where the beef cattle feedlots were located in relation to the swine.

Men came and went from the building, as there were sleeping rooms and cots for the employees and cattlemen. No one seemed to take notice of his lounging presence. Bakeries and cafeterias were inside, and he decided to enter and go directly to the men's room. Removing his tie, he placed a silver dollar in one of the ends. As he waited, he tested its weight until the movement was set in his mind. He moved to behind the entrance door and waited. The door swung open, and he was ready as a medium-sized railroad man stepped inside.

Stepping from behind the door, he swung the improvised garrote around the man's neck and deftly caught the weighted end with his other hand. He quickly twisted the tie, cutting off the man's exclamations of surprise.

With practiced ease, he slammed his knee into his victim's back. With a sudden jerk of his wrists, he broke the man's neck with a sickening crunch. The death was quick. The captain forced a wedge under the door to keep it closed and dragged the dead man to the stall. He quickly stripped the man, then donned the stolen clothes.

With the bag over his shoulder and wearing the uniform of a railroad employee, he headed toward the outside.

Just as he was about to step outside, he noticed the shadows of two people. He stopped and watched as the two walked in front of the door. He sunk back and waited as they entered the main lobby doors.

"Ron and Brita," he told himself. Complete the mission first, he told himself, and kill them later.

If Ron discovered the body, it would work to his advantage. The police would be too busy to notice someone hovering near the elevators.

When he thought they were out of sight, he stepped out from behind the wall.

*****

Ron and Brita stayed near the bakery, watching as people came and went from the many facilities. Neither had seen Swensen for a short while, and Ron became worried. Brita went to the women's restroom located on opposite ends of the large room. Ron waited near the men's in case Swensen had gone in to relieve himself.

When Brita made eye contact, he motioned that he was going to enter the men's room.

Chapter Seventeen

After a few minutes of scanning the room, Brita nervously jammed her fist in her gun pocket and hiked toward the men's restroom. The same nauseated feeling that she'd had at the time of Mindel's death swept through her. *It never takes a man this long,* she reasoned. Something must be wrong. Her heart almost dropped to her knees when guilt started to inch into her soul. Two murders, Rose and Mindel, because she'd been too slow and indecisive? What about Charlot Fortier? Could she have prevented his disappearance? Brita couldn't let it happen again. She *wouldn't* let it happen again.

Brita wrapped her palm around the derringer and glanced around the foyer in search of anything out of the ordinary. Her mind buzzed with fear and anxiety as sweat beads popped out on her brow. A mixture of relief and distress spread through her when she realized the person who'd stepped out from behind a counter wasn't Swensen. Still, no one came out of the men's room. Brita became certain that the worst was happening, and knew that she had to act immediately. Just as she was about to approach the restroom door, an older gentleman came up behind her, headed for the men's room.

"Sir?" She trembled with fear. "I'd like to know if my brother is still inside the restroom. His name is Ron. He's tall, with light brown hair. Would you please have a look in and tell me?" Brita gave him a smile that would melt butter. She felt like she was deceiving her grandpa.

"You bet, just wait a sec," he said, chuckling.

The door swung shut as Brita waited for what seemed like an hour. Brita glanced up to the ceiling and ran her sweaty palms up and down her arms, wondering what was taking so long. She stared at the clock, which had ticked by a full two minutes. That was long enough, she thought. Suddenly the gentleman stepped out, looking white as a ghost.

"Is he in…" Brita's question trailed off as she touched the man's arm.

"No time, lady." He brushed off her hand. Brita could only watch as he dashed up the stairs. "Ron?" She entered the men's room, closing the door behind her. "Where are you?" She was about to leave when he kicked the stall door open.

"Don't come any closer," Ron hissed. He was annoyed, yet relieved to see her—even though she hadn't listened and was still walking toward him. He'd been studying the undressed body, calculating all the known information about Rose's murder, and comparing it to the one in front of him. He'd been about to try and open the man's mouth to see if a silver dollar was inside of it when the gentleman had walked in.

"I can't believe it." Brita felt lightheaded and the room seemed to spin under her feet, and she leaned against the wall. "This is all my fault." Her shoulders slumped as her eyes filled with tears.

"He was already dead when I came in." Ron sighed and stood up. "We'd better get out of here, NOW!" He'd had enough time to study the body, and concluded that the method used on this latest victim was the same that had been used on Rose. This time the tie had been left behind, and there was a trace of makeup on it—perhaps from Rose. If his hunch was right, then Swensen had killed at least two people using a tie as a murder weapon.

Ron ground his teeth and rubbed his chin as he began trying to decipher why Swensen needed the man's clothes. The dead man's face was swollen and purple, giving no clue as to his identity or occupation. His hands were callused and seamed with black, and his fingernails were filled with the same black material. Scars from burns flecked the back of his hands and arms.

A railroad fireman. So Swensen must now be walking

around in a pair of railroad overalls. What was in Omaha that Swensen needed to infiltrate wearing such a disguise?

Suddenly, the newspaper article surfaced in his mind, the one about the large die-off of German cattle caused by some kind of toxin in the feed. If enough toxin was eaten by the animals, they lose weight and become violently ill. Time seemed to stop as he came to the frightening realization that everything was linked together. Margot's death. Her notes about the laboratory project on grain toxins. And Swensen being in Minneapolis, Chicago, and Omaha.

"My God!" Ron's eyes flashed wide open.

"What are you thinking?" Brita asked, his clipped tone making her jump. She was wiping her eyes and trying to catch her breath after yet another death she had failed to stop.

"I'm thinking that we'd better get out of here and go separately so if one of us is caught, the other can still take care of the situation." He steered her toward the door. "He's dressed as a railroad man, and he might be by the elevators. We can't let him near the grates. He's going to poison the feed." He kissed her gently. "Go, now before he makes it to the intake grate! I'll be right behind. We'll meet at the elevators. If you happen to see me with the cops, just look the other way."

"Got it." Opening the door, Brita glanced over at the body and shuddered. "Just like…"

"Rose." Ron finished. "Hurry, before the cops come." A terrible sense of dread overcame him as he thought about Margot, and now Brita. He couldn't lose her too, because it would kill him.

Trembling with fear, Brita slipped out. Nervous and filled with anxiety, she hurried for the stairs, which led to the main level. It took just a short time to reach the stone arches outside.

Brita studied the grounds, and was thankful that the sun was beginning to rise. On her left stood the police station, but it was at least one if not two blocks behind the yards. She studied the skyline in search of the railroad towers. Lining the block were several packing plants, and various companies had buildings dotting the perimeter. Brita slipped her hands in her pockets to make sure that the gun and knife hadn't disappeared. She drew in a few deep breaths and formulated a quick plan before climbing down the stairs leading into the street.

*****

Ron looked for a different route out. He went to the stall and raised himself up on the toilet seat. There was a window up above, which was painted shut. He dug his keys from his pocket, and scraped along the window frame until the paint cracked. With a sharp snap, he opened it. Climbing on top of the toilet tank, he maneuvered his upper torso up onto the window ledge and pulled himself out, just as the bathroom door opened and voices rose from the room.

"Stop him!" a police officer shouted when they heard the window bang shut.

"Shit!" Ron growled and hurried away. He pulled his collar up to shield his face and smoothed his hair over so that it parted on the opposite side.

He was worried sick about Brita, but knew that she'd be better off without him. All that mattered was finding Swensen. A sense of foreboding hung over him like a dark cloud as he considered the panic that poisoned cattle and swine would set off, and the resulting blow to the war effort.

Ron glanced up and saw the railroad tower. The fastest route was almost in a straight line. Walking briskly, he headed right toward it. Two policemen rounded the corner in front of him and nudged each other. Ron turned in the other direction and began to run.

"Stop!" one of the policeman shouted. Both ran after him, blowing their whistles. Two other policemen rushed down the building stairs, and another came through the window and was hot on Ron's heels. A railroad bull stepped out from the side fencing and stood with his arms crossed and legs spread wide apart like a sentry post. Ron knew it was going to be impossible to bypass him without hurting him.

Ron debated whether to give up or not. He was certain that he'd be able to talk himself out of the mess in a short time, and then he'd be able to find Brita and locate Swensen. When a policeman raised his pistol to fire at him, Ron stopped in his tracks.

"You got me," Ron shouted, raising his hands.

*****

Brita kept running, falling a few times in the straw that blew on the ground from the trucks. For as far as she could see or hear there was nothing but animal tails and horns and squeals. The noise was deafening. Despite it—and the stench—she wound closer to the pens, looking for an elevator that would raise the animals and move them from pen to pen. She stood on top of hay bales for a moment with her hands on her hips, and stared until finally giving up her search for a stock elevator.

The yard lights beamed like tiny stars, and Brita gazed up at the horizon. In big bold letters across the tallest building, UNITED FIELDS GRAIN ELEVATOR was printed. "Idiot!" Brita growled, slapping a palm on her forehead when she realized that he had meant a grain elevator. As she started running toward it, Brita made a solemn vow to never tell a single soul her mistake, especially not Ron. She wondered how long it would take for him to catch up to her.

Some kid's bike was left by a yard gate, and there were newspapers stacked on the ground right beside it. Delivery boy, she mused, hustling over to it. "Sorry, she mumbled as she climbed on to it, pedaling away.

At last the elevator chute came into view. The railroad tower, which directed the flow of the grain cars, was right across the street. Brita jumped off the bike as soon as she was close to the tower. She dropped the bike and studied the men gathered near a large grate. *Is that what he meant?*

Brita's nerves prickled, and sweat trickled down the back of her neck. *Where is he,* she wondered, but knew that the killer's gait would be distinct in her mind. She glanced up and saw the South Omaha switching. Brita scanned all of the men. A policeman walked by, and Brita began to feel uncomfortable. She stayed near the guard tower and watched all the men around the elevators. No one stuck out above the rest. There was a man about Swensen's size, but he had a limp. Then she wondered if it wasn't him when the guard held up his lantern and pointed to a spot across the street.

Frowning, Brita hiked to the opposite side and stood behind a large oak tree, looking toward the Swift and Company buildings. Near the far corner, she saw someone leaning against the building and lighting a cigarette. Her heart pounded. From the glow of the match Brita knew, and she fumbled to get the derringer out of her pocket… and she made sure the safety was off.

Her knees felt shaky as she crossed the vacant lot toward him.

"Don't move or I'll shoot!" she stammered. She approached him from his blind side.

*****

"Hand cuff 'im," the elder police officer ordered. "We don't want a killer on the loose."

"Yes, sir." The younger officer cuffed Ron's hands behind his back. "You're coming with me." He started to nudge Ron toward the police station.

"I didn't kill anyone, and you're letting the real killer escape. I can explain who I am later."

The two men in blue chuckled.

"You're a real clown," the younger officer snickered.

"Off to the station," the elder officer growled. "Our sergeant is going to be pleased with us." He gave himself a smile and a nod for finding the killer so fast.

"Put him in the cell," the elder policeman said when they walked in the door. "I'll go and tell the sergeant that we have our man."

"Yes, sir," the younger policeman said. He shoved Ron down the hallway.

Once they'd reached the cell, the officer pushed him in roughly. "Against the wall."

"I keep telling you, you've got the wrong man."

"Shaddup!" The policeman shoved Ron asked the wall and began to search him.

"Call this number." Ron snapped off the telephone number for Washington. "It'll explain everything."

"Shaddup!"

Ron felt like a ninny. When he was asked to remove his shirt and was patted down for weapons and searched for identification, the officer noticed all kinds of red lipstick marks around his neck.

The policeman threw Ron his clothes after finishing the search. "Get dressed. We're going to see Sergeant Sinclair."

"Let's hope your sergeant will listen to reason," Ron grumbled as he dressed.

"This way, Lover Boy."

"It's Captain Ron Healy." Ron made sure that his posture was distinctly military.

The policeman opened the door, and the elder officer did the talking. "Sergeant, here's the prisoner." He handed the notebook with all the questions and answers and particulars written in it over to the sergeant.

"Send him in," Sergeant Sinclair ordered. Ron's commanding presence took him by surprise. The sergeant stood up and glanced at the sheets of paper. "Good job, boys. I think we got our man," he said to the officers. He cocked his head and gave Ron a sly grin as he continued reading.

"Well, Lover Boy, what have you to say for yourself?" Sergeant Sinclair asked, plunking his girth down into his chair. "Tell me about the lipstick. Why you don't have any identification on you? Why did you run from my boys as soon as you saw them? Why I shouldn't book you for murder right this minute?" He leaned over his desk with a beetle brow and stared at Ron. "Well? I'm dying to know."

"The lipstick is from my girl, Brita Torgerson. If you'd just call the Washington number that I gave to the officers during the interrogation, they will explain everything." Ron kept his anger at bay by breathing slow and deep. "There's a killer on the loose, and I know who it is and where he's at. Send two or three or a dozen of your men to follow me… if I'm wrong, then shoot me." Ron stood at military attention. "You have to believe me."

"Did you see anyone else inside the men's room when you entered?" The sergeant rubbed his chin as he held his pencil poised to write.

"I didn't see a soul. The man who did it is using the name Swensen. He rode the Twin Cities Zephyr, then the Chicago-Denver line." Annoyed, Ron felt his jaw muscles start to flinch. "Either you let me go, or I'll drop the wrath of the US Army on your ass. I am an OSS agent assigned to the Zephyr." He cleared his throat and took in a deep breath, keeping his eyes steady on the sergeant. "If you were to send someone to the Zephyr and ask the conductor to take you to my room, you will find my identification. My orders are strictly confidential, sir." Ron damned himself for not bothering to pick up his papers and gun. He hoped that the thick-headed sergeant would pay attention to him before it was too late. "Please trust me, sir."

"Go make that phone call," the sergeant ordered one of the officers, then turned back to Ron. "Do you realize that it's six o'clock in the morning in Washington? My boss will have my ass if this gets back to him." He pursed his fat lips like a big red fireball.

"Might as well have a seat and relax. We're going to be awhile." The sergeant scratched his whiskers as he peered at Ron and waited for him to take a seat. "Now take it from the top, and help my too-slow mind catch up. Who is this Brita? Your accomplice, the one with the red lipstick?"

"My orders are confidential. You can contact three-star General Torgerson and he'll clear me. Let's just say that I'm here to make sure the Zephyr and its employees and passengers are safe. That should explain to you why we were together." Ron shook his head, glanced at the clock before starting his long speech. "Brita's safety is part of my assignment, and if anything happens to her…" Ron shook his head.

"I still haven't been brought up to the present. I'm waiting." The sergeant cupped his ear, as if his patience were wearing thin.

"When the general explained my orders, he also spoke of a dear friend who had gone missing, and has since been found dead. I met up with the Zephyr in Chicago and have been working undercover as the bartender. There have been two murders since I began my duty. First one was in Chicago—gunshot wound to the head. The second was in Burlington, Iowa… a woman was strangled using a garrote, and a silver dollar was left in her mouth. I'm not sure what the motive was, but I'm positive that it was the same killer." He glanced at the clock and noted that time had indeed ticked by. He suddenly felt on edge. "What's taking the officer who was making the phone call so long? He should've been back here by now. It's been over thirty minutes."

"Protocol. You know, there's the assistants and aides, and they have to decide if they should wake the general…that is, if there truly is a general." He stared at Ron, furrowing his brow. "And there had better damn well be one, because your story is awfully far-fetched and full of holes. The ties don't make any sense, nor the lipstick," he growled, banging his fist on the desktop. "And none of it explains the murder here."

"Call the lipstick a lack of discretion." Ron took in a deep breath and blew it out before continuing. "I think this man, Swensen, is going to poison the livestock. I have reason to believe…"

"You're really stretching it to the limit, buddy." The sergeant growled and banged his fist on the desk, which caused the files to shift. At the same moment, the door started to squeak open. He looked toward the policeman entering the room.

"I have news," the officer said, glancing at his sergeant and then over to Ron. He hesitated when he noticed that his sergeant was on the edge of his chair and the once neat stacks of paper were ready to tip. Anxious, he reached out with the notebook. "Sarge?"

"Yes? What is it?" the sergeant snapped. "It's about time. It's been darn near an hour. Now give it to me." He snatched the notebook from the officer's hand and glanced at them. "Now get to the Zephyr and speed those guys up. That's an order!"

"Yes, sir." The young officer fled the room.

"Well, Captain Ron Healy, it appears that you may be telling the truth. However, we still need picture identification." He studied the notes before raising his beady eyes to Ron. "There's just one more thing."

"Well? What is it?" Ron sat straighter. He suddenly felt a surge of energy at the possibility that his story would finally be believed. "Please, hurry. The trail is getting colder by the second."

"Not so fast," the sergeant said, stone faced. "What's your code phrase?"

"Code phrase? I wasn't assigned one. What are you talking about?" Ron shook his head. "Code phrase?"

"You'd better come with me." The sergeant got up, came around the desk, and grabbed Ron by the shoulder. "You're being booked right now," he growled. "I hate liars." He started to pull Ron to his feet.

"Wait a minute. Give me time to think, will ya?" Ron wanted to bash him in the chops, because none of it made any sense. He hadn't been assigned a code phrase. He wondered… could it be possible? His fingers started to ache when he thought of Brita; how luscious her kisses were, how soft she felt, her moonbeam-drenched hair, her long legs… and finally he sighed. "I know what it is… it has to be…" he concluded. Raising his eyes to the sergeant, he smiled ruefully. "Fucking fingers. As in, 'I will break all ten of your fucking fingers if you touch my daughter.'" Ron waited for a moment as the officer and the sergeant looked at each other. "Right?"

"That explains the lipstick." The sergeant chuckled as he opened the door and hollered down the hall. "Officers Anderson and Odegaard, ASAP!" He looked over at Ron. "No gun until we get a picture identification on you. The officers will have orders to shoot you if you try running." He studied Ron.

"I understand."

"Good." At that moment, the two officers entered the room. The sergeant glanced at the clock. "Over an hour has passed… the killer has that much time on us. You are to follow Captain Healy. However, there's a catch. He doesn't have a gun, and if he tries to run, then shoot him. Understood?"

"Yes, sir," they said in unison.

"Let's hurry." Ron had started toward the door when a tall officer and a short, stubby one stepped into the room.

"Here's his identification," the red-headed officer said, handing it to the sergeant.

"Good." The sergeant glanced at Ron, then studied the picture. "Well? What are you waiting for? There's a killer loose! Give Captain Healy a gun," he snapped, handing Ron back his identification.

Finally, Ron thought, as they headed out the door.

He snatched the gun the officer handed him, and explained about the mission as they ran out the door.

"The quickest route to the elevator is this way," Officer Odegaard said. "Follow me."

Chapter Eighteen

Captain Arnwolf glanced at his watch before looking up at the tower. Men dressed in railroad overalls were walking out of the gates as others came in. With the shift change, he had time for a quick cigarette, and set the satchel down beside him. Everything had gone so smoothly. The mission was complete—except for killing the general's brat.

"Don't move, or I'll shoot!"

Startled, he turned to see the brat with straw sticking out of her hair, ripped clothes… and a derringer aimed at his chest. He cursed himself for not killing her when he'd had the chance. Her aim looked as steady as a poker player dealt a royal flush.

"I mean it! I'll shoot!" She took another step closer to him, her grip firming on her weapon.

He inhaled deeply and slowly inched backward, not stopping until the yard lights couldn't reach him. He kept his eye on her trigger finger while holding his cigarette steady. His mind raced with possibilities until he decided what course to follow.

"Ah, Brita. What are you doing out here at this hour of the night, eh?" He took a drag from his cigarette, and noticed that her hands shook less.

"Shut up!" she shouted. She continued to step closer.

"Now Brita, don't be so harsh," he murmured. He tried to draw her in closer. "Want a cigarette?" He stared into her eyes as she inched forward.

"Stop trying to distract me." She held the gun steady and walked toward him. "Come out in the open!"

"Everyone is allowed one last request." He grinned and took another drag from his cigarette.

"Killer!" Brita took another step forward. Her eyes opened wide with shock when he flicked his cigarette towards her face. She flinched as the cherry skimmed her cheek, causing her to waver and her hands to clench.

Swensen quickly reached for the gun as she pulled the trigger. "Bitch!" The bullet struck his foot. Ignoring the pain, he reached for the gun as it dropped to the ground and skidded. Swensen bit back German curses as he fumbled to reach for it. At the same time, Brita kicked it out into the street. They collided and fell together in a heap.

Holding a kerosene lamp, the tower guard looked over a ledge and witnessed a man and woman fighting. "What's going on down there? Leave her alone!" A shot fired, and the guard reached for his pistol, aiming at the couple. "Let her go!" He raised the tower emergency arm.

Swensen grabbed Brita's hair and pulled her in front of him as a shield, then rolled to his feet.

"Shoot me, and I'll shoot her," he growled. He pulled her toward the derringer and hoped the idiot couldn't see that he was still unarmed.

"Give yourself up!" The tower guard held the pistol steady on the two, watching as the woman wrestled with her captor.

Brita jammed her right elbow back into Swensen's gut, which made him flinch and release his hold. She drove her heel into his wounded foot, twisted around and planted her knee into his groin.

"*Du Nutte!*" he cried, doubling over in pain.

"Shoot him! Shoot him!" she screamed. Frantically, she searched for the gun.

Both sighted the derringer at the same time and dove for it simultaneously. Brita grabbed it first and pulled the trigger, the bullet hitting him on the side of the neck. Swensen slumped into a heap as he grabbed his jugular.

"Oh my God!" She dropped the gun when the blood spurting between Swensen's fingers splattered onto her.

An oncoming train whistle blew in the distance. The tower

guard began waving another flag.

"You okay?" he hollered down to her.

Brita stood motionless, staring as Swensen's lifeblood escaped his body. Realizing that the gun was still within his reach, she bent toward him to pick it up.

"Der Mohr hat seine Schuldigkeit getan…" Swensen said softly. His eyes glazed over.

"What?" Brita held her breath as she leaned closer to his mouth.

"Alles is vorbei." Swensen's eyes fluttered.

Brita waited until he shut them for the last time. She tried to shake his cold, accusing eyes from her mind, and shuddered as she stared down at his lifeless body. After a moment of silence, she tried to make sense of what he'd said. When the tower guard yelled down to her, it jolted her back to the moment.

"When they see the sign that I have hanging out from the tower, the police will come running. Just stay put little lady, I'll be there in a moment."

Brita nodded as fear and anxiety began to leave her body. She sank to the ground, bowed her head and rocked back and forth, wrapping her arms around her knees. Tears streamed down her face. She became suddenly aware of the awful stench that she smelled after awaking from Mindel's murder. She looked at Swensen with hate, but still felt guilty for not preventing Mindel's murder.

A train whistle in the distance didn't disrupt her self-inflicted guilt. Startled, she felt the soft touch of the tower guard's hand on her shoulder.

"Ma'am, don't fret. Everything'll be just fine." The tower guard reached down gently and held out his hand to her. When Brita placed her hand in his, he raised her to standing. "Don't worry, the police will soon be here. I have to return to the tower to re-direct the trains, but I wanted to make sure that you're all right." He looked into the red-rimmed eyes, and sighed. "Here," he said softly. Reaching into his pocket, he handed her a clean handkerchief. "Blow."

"Thanks." Brita sniffled and wiped her nose. "Do you want it back?" she stammered, unsure of what to do or say. The tower guard looked pleasant and concerned, which made her want to start to cry all over again.

"Keep it." He brushed her hand away. "I've got plenty more. Time to buck up, kid," he grouched so that she'd quit crying. "Clean yourself up before the gawkers get here."

"Why didn't you shoot?" Brita asked. It suddenly became clear to her that she could've been the dead one, not Swensen. Anger swept through her. "He almost killed me. I could be dead right now. That could be me lying there and not him!" She pointed at Swensen. "Why?" She narrowed her brow and glared him. To bite back the tears, she clamped her jaw tight. The last thing she needed to do was cry, again.

"I didn't have any bullets," he said sheepishly. "I'm sorry. I did all that I could do. I cleaned the gun after using it for target practice yesterday with my son." He drew in a deep breath. "I'm your witness. I know that you killed him in self-defense."

"I'm sorry, I didn't mean to snap at you. Now I've got to remember what his dying words were. They were in German." She silently massaged her temples. Brita's nerves were still jangled and adrenaline pumped through her system like a lightning rod. She trembled deep inside, forcing herself to look away so that he wouldn't be able to see her turn red from nervousness. "Be brave," her daddy would say. Brita glanced over to the spot where Swensen had been smoking his cigarette, and she saw his satchel.

His final word had been "done." It didn't make any sense to her at all as she tried to recall what Ron had said about the elevators. It sounded like a puzzle that was missing a few pieces. She shook her head and let out a long breath. Brita ran her fingers through her hair to help her think as pieces of straw and grass fell to the ground.

"I've gotta go, little miss. Are you gonna be okay?" The guard spoke soft and clear as he spotted an approaching train.

"Thank you. Yes… ah… I don't even know your name. I'm

Brita." Her mind started to settle as the shock began to wear off.

"Scott." He hurried away to resume his duties.

Brita mulled Swensen's last words over in her mind. She walked toward the satchel, which was sitting a few yards away.

Before touching the handle, Brita took in a deep breath to steady her nerves. "The deed's done" churned in her head, as well as what Ron had said about the elevators and the poisoning of the German beef supply. Nothing made any sense, she thought as she hesitantly began to open the bag.

Pawing through the satchel, she discovered a set of clothes, cigarettes, and three different passports. They showed nationalities from Denmark, Poland and the USA. Each picture was doctored just a little — with glasses or facial hair — but Brita knew for sure that it was Swensen. The mole on his left ear that looked like an earring was never disguised. As she lifted out a thermos, Brita realized how light it was and decided it must be empty.

The noise from the elevator chute intruded on her inspection. She looked over toward it. A couple of men were busy with brooms, sweeping spilled grain into the grates, oblivious to the drama that had just played out moments before. Brita's heart began to pound like a drum as she suddenly realized one of the puzzle pieces had something to do with the elevator, and thought of the corn kernels.

Brita began waving her arms and yelling for them to stop.

Three men looked up and saw some woman who looked like a scarecrow waving and jumping up and down. "What on earth is wrong with her?" one of them asked.

As she began running across the street toward them, approaching sirens screamed. She turned to see two squad cars roaring up the street. When they suddenly screeched to a halt, she hoped Ron was inside one of them. Her heart finally started to beat normally.

A couple of policemen stopped by the body, and Brita watched as one of them leaned over and felt Swensen's neck.

She was just about to walk over to them when she noticed Ron start racing toward the elevators.

Brita's eyes opened wide when she saw that he was carrying a gun, but figured it was for self-protection.

"I'm over here!" She jumped up and down. "It's about time that you got here!" Brita started running to him.

*****

"Don't touch the elevator," Ron shouted. When he finally reached it, he turned his back to Brita and ordered, "Don't touch anything!" Then he flipped open his badge. "OSS Agent Healy. Drop your tools, NOW!" He could tell by the way that they looked at him, with the gun in his hand that they weren't sure what to think.

"Drop what you're doing, boys. Go take a break," an unrecognized officer said. He stood ramrod stiff and held their gaze until they set down the gear.

"Stay right here, and don't move until we get this figured out." Ron ordered, staring at them. He slipped the gun into his shoulder holster and made a mental note to thank George when he returned to the station for remembering to bring it.

*****

Brita stopped just short of swinging him around to face her, but her mouth dropped in disbelief when she saw his badge. She'd thought he was just a bartender, only to find out that he was an OSS agent. It made her wonder what else she didn't know about him. Crossing her arms, she glared at him.

"Hi to you, too," she growled. When Ron didn't look her way, she balled her fists and jammed them into her pockets.

"I'm busy. Not now," Ron snapped, avoiding her eyes.

Grabbing Ron's arm, she swung him around. "What took you so damn long? I could've been killed while you've been lollygagging around, rounding up a posse."

"No time for that story." Ron glanced at the two policemen who were examining Swensen. "You killed him?" She nodded.

"How?"

"There was a struggle. The tower guard can give you the details, he saw it all." She crossed her arms and glared at him.

"Any last words? Where's his satchel?"

"It's over across the street by that building," she answered, nodding toward it. "I was just pawing through it when I saw those men beginning to work around the elevator. Then you came." She almost choked on her words, because his deception disgusted her so much.

"What did he say? Anything at all that you remember?" He waited for an answer. "Well? It wasn't that long ago." Ron looked at the officer beside him. "Go and get it." He turned back to Brita and spoke through clenched teeth. "I'm waiting… I haven't got all day…"

"Shutup! For your information, it was all in German. Give me a damn minute, will you? It's not as if it's my native tongue, you idiot!" she snapped. Brita wanted to bash him in the noggin just to show him that she was a person.

"His last words were *Du Nutte. Der Mohr hat seine Schuldigkeit getan*. Oh yes… there were a couple more words…"

"It's important… hurry up!" Ron growled.

"*Alles is vorbei*." She glared at him and saw red. "You figure it out, Mr. Smarty Pants," Brita answered sarcastically. "What took you so damn long?" She pushed her hands in her pockets and balled her fists.

"Not now," Ron hissed. He turned to the elevator as he repeated the German.

"I'm just fine by the way," she snapped to his back. "Thank you for asking, and for your consideration." Brita gave him one last glare as the officer returned carrying the satchel. She had a vague idea where the police station was, and started walking toward it.

Ron began searching the contents of the satchel. The clothes went to the ground immediately. He looked at officer Odegaard. "Wait. I want you to take all of this back to the station." The passports were of greater interest, and he opened them. Poland, Denmark, and the US. "Shit! Shoulda known."

"What, sir?" Odegaard asked, leaning closer to hear.

"Nothing." He shook his head, dropping the passports and the wallet into Odegaard's other hand.

When Ron picked up the empty thermos, he understood the true meaning of Swensen's last words. The grain had been compromised.

"Shit!" He shifted back to the three men. "Why the hell are you guys still here? Get the manager, NOW!" He turned to Odegaard. "Get Sinclair out here! We need more officers to guard the elevators. Go! Take all of this back with you immediately, and don't let it out of your sight." Ron stuffed everything but the thermos back into the satchel and handed it to him. "GO! Give this to the OSS agent, George Gullickson."

"Yes, sir," Officer Odegaard replied. He turned and headed for the nearest squad car.

Ron looked up toward the sky and gave himself a moment to collect his thoughts. The thermos was tucked in the crook of his arm and was going to stay there until he could figure out what to do with it. He didn't want to trust it to anyone except a scientist who could figure out what sort of poison had been inside of it before they could locate it in the grain. Looking back towards Swensen's body as it was being lifted onto a stretcher, Ron saw an officer talking with a man built like a beanpole and wearing a railroad set of overalls. He walked over to them.

"What have you got?" Ron studied the man.

"Sir? I have an eye witness here," Officer Olson said. "Scott, the tower guard. He can tell you what happened."

"Good. In the meantime, I want this entire section roped off. No trains or trucks of any kind in or out."

When Olson left, Ron looked at Scott. "Did you see if he spilled anything—anything at all—into grates, trucks, chutes, pens… anything?" Ron was wishing against all odds that the man might be able to tell him what had happened with the poison.

"No, sorry. I just saw the struggle. I didn't see him do

anything. I can't help you there." Scott shook his head. "I wish I knew what you were after. Maybe I could be of more help." He reached into his front pocket, took out his railroad watch and read it, listened for a second, shut the face-cover, then jammed it back into his front pocket. "The signal was red. There will be no trains coming for a while." He nodded to himself.

"Did you see him near the elevator chute?" Ron watched him shake his head. "A grain truck? The weigh station? Think. Where did you see him? Take your time. Think, man, think."

Scott pressed his chin into the palm of right hand and closed his eyes.

The highest ranking detective finished taking statements from the three men, then looked at Ron. "I'll take his next," he said, nodding to the guard.

"Give him a minute," Ron said softly, going over to him. "I need to know if he saw the victim near anything before the scuffle began. It's more important than anything else. Tell me immediately. Got that?"

"Yes," the officer said, nodding. "Understood."

"Good."

"I've got to speak with the elevator manager. I think that's him coming." Ron motioned to a short, thick-set man who looked like a barrel. "Interrupt me if you find out any more details."

"Understood," the detective replied.

Ron steered the manager over toward the building where they'd find privacy.

Initially, Ron gave him an excuse for not starting the elevator because of the murder. He didn't want to start a panic by saying more. After explaining what he could, Ron questioned him about whether he'd seen anyone lurking about during the night. Unfortunately, the manager had just come on duty. Exasperated, Ron let out a long breath and wished that he smoked, because it would be a good time for a cigarette. Glancing over his shoulder, he saw a newspaper reporter shout out questions. Ron clenched his jaw and thought of man-eating menaces.

"Stay right where you are," Ron ordered the manager as he started walking toward the detective.

"Yes, sir."

The detective, sensing the urgency, hurried over after writing Scott's statement down.

"I've got something, sir," he said, shaking the pad. "I think you're gonna like it." Olson ran toward Ron.

"Let's hear it," Ron said, his heart pumping hard from anxiety and fear. "Did he see Swensen anywhere?" He expected the worst, but hoped for the best.

"Yes. The girl noticed him standing by the building smoking, but before that..." he said as he flipped his page.

"Yes?" Ron snapped while clutching Olson's arm.

"The intake grates. That's where Scott first saw him before he went across the street. Didn't see him again until Brita came." He flipped his notepad closed and stuffed it into his breast pocket.

"Now we have a starting point. I think the grain is compromised. We must get the university to send out their top researchers in organic chemistry. Do it now. There's no time to waste."

"Yes, sir. I'm right on it, sir," he said.

Ron went over to the manager. "I want you to explain how this works. Please make it as succinct and understandable as possible. And make it quick."

"Yes, sir." The manager looked at him. "Follow me!"

Ron listened and watched as the manager pointed to the different parts of the elevator, explaining how it worked.

"After it's decided what bin the grain goes into, whether a boxcar surge bin or a farmer's truck, it's loaded by a series of buckets to the top of the elevator where it's stored. The elevator maintains a cool temperature because it can become combustible from the heat of the grain drying out. From there, the grain travels through a series of spouts until it's sent to its proper bin for storage. Each bin holds different grades of wheat.

"When the wheat is shipped or moved, it is sent to a different loading bin that is called a hopper. From there the grain is sent through into the cleaner bin. After it's been cleaned, it's sent to another hopper where it's surged into a separate hopper or boxcar and is shipped out."

"Thanks," Ron said. He still was trying to understand it all. "Stay within this area in case we need further explanations. No one is to touch anything, including you." Ron studied him. "Understood?"

"Understood. But what does this have to do with the murder?" His eyes opened wide as he stared into Ron's eyes.

"Everything." Ron gave him an even stare. "He may have poisoned the grain, that's why the bins have to be protected."

"I understand. I'll tell my men to steer clear until this has been resolved. I'll be in my office."

"Thank you."

Ron watched him walk away before switching his attention to the crime scene and walking over toward it.

The coroner was just about to drive away. Ron took one last look at Swensen.

"Okay," he said after he'd flipped back the blanket and looked at Swensen's face. When the car rolled away, Brita crossed his mind.

"Where's Brita?" he asked the nearest policeman.

"Brita who?"

"Where is she? How could she leave without permission?" Ron swore under his breath, and glanced around the policemen. He kept his eyes open for a blonde, but only saw the uniform blue colors. Next, he walked over to where they'd last spoken and looked around, suddenly realizing that she must be really angry. "I'm going after her. So help me, I'll find her and she's going to listen to reason."

Chapter Nineteen

Day Six

With her fists balled in her pockets, Brita marched toward the police station, oblivious to her surroundings. *Can't trust a man,* she told herself, confirming it with a nod. She should've known that he was some kind of an agent, now that she thought about the manner in which they'd met. It was too coincidental. A bartender walking the rails and accidentally coming across her in the middle of the night. The story was really too stupid to be believed. She berated herself for falling for his good looks and charm, when all he was concerned about was keeping tabs on her. She realized that her dad put him up to looking after her like a little girl who didn't know what to do.

The sun's rays were rising behind the tall Exchange Building, and Brita stopped to look where she was going. Officer Odegaard pulled the squad car right along beside her. He leaned over to the side window and called to her. "Jump in. I'm going to the station. We have to take your statement before you can resume your duties on the train."

"Oh…well… I already knew that," she grouched. Brita stepped to the opened door and crawled inside. "I want to get this over with." Brita glanced out at the stockyards, and suddenly the noise became deafening. She plugged her ears to block out the sound.

Brita had never seen so many heads of cattle or heard so many pigs oink n her life and she hoped that she'd never have to see any again for a long time. One pen was no different from the other when it came to distinguishing the smell. She pinched her nose and prayed that they'd soon reach the station. It made her appreciate city life. It was a relief when they'd rounded the final pen, skirted along the outside of it, and turned the corner.

"We're almost there," Officer Odegaard said, matter-of-factly. He noticed her gray complexion. "You're not going to faint from the smell, are you?"

"Not on your life," she snapped. "I'm fine." There was no way on earth that she'd ever trust another man with knowing her thoughts or weaknesses.

Turning the final corner, the station came into plain view.

Casually she lifted her arm and muffled a gasp—she reeked of sweat and who knew what else. Raking her fingers through her hair, she hoped that it would help her appearance but she didn't know how to hide her smell. Grinning to herself, she decided it didn't matter since the stench of the stockyards would mask it.

When Odegaard had parked the car, Brita reached for the door handle.

"Just a minute, Miss Torgerson." He came around to open the door for her. "You've been through quite an ordeal. This way, miss."

He led her up the few stairs inside of the small police station.

As they walked toward the sergeant's office, she glanced at the clock. It was five o'clock in the morning, and she had just enough time to make the last leg of the journey to Denver.

"May I go to the women's room?" Brita asked. "I really have to go." She started balancing from one foot to the next. "It's a must."

"Sure," he answered. "Right this way." He nodded to the door. "I'll wait right here."

"It'll just take a minute," she said, yawning. Once inside the room, Brita quickly headed for the sink and mirror. She picked the straw from her hair before trying to smooth it down with her fingers. Cupping her hands under the water, she gave herself a quick splash-up wash. Her eyes looked like a road map, but there wasn't anything that she could do about it.

When she finished, she put a smile on her face before heading out into the hallway.

"Right this way," Officer Odegaard said. He led her to the sergeant's office.

The police sergeant sat behind his desk, but someone else she recognized sat opposite him. It was the passenger who'd reminded her of a gangster, George.

Both looked over as she stood there.

"Sergeant, I have Miss Torgerson," Officer Odegaard said. "Also, Captain Healy needs more men to cordon off the elevator, and he'd like for you to come and discuss a certain matter with him."

"Miss Torgerson, have a seat." Sergeant Sinclair motioned to the open chair. "You've been through quite an ordeal over the last few days, I hear. Unfortunately, we need to get a statement from you." He gave her a reassuring smile.

"Does my father know about Ron Healy?" she asked. "How do you fit into this, George?"

"I'm Agent Gullickson—I'm from the OSS, as is Captain Healy," George spoke quietly, then leaned toward her. "We were as a matter of fact, assigned to keep an eye out for Nazi infiltrators traveling on the Zephyr. It was a matter of national security. But your father asked Agent Healy to keep a close eye on you as well. He wants you to return to Washington as soon as possible."

"Then it is true about Ron… I mean Captain Healy," she murmured. Suddenly it dawned on her what he'd just said. "Captain Healy was assigned to watch over me as a bodyguard? Nazi infiltrators? This all sounds too farfetched." She suppressed her anger. "I'm continuing to Denver." She forced herself to calm down and not let anyone see how truly upset she was. "I'm doing what I want to do, period."

"I understand. I'll contact the general to keep him informed. Ron was not your bodyguard; the general was concerned because of the Nazi infiltrators, and he worried about your friend, Dr. Fortier."

"It's time to get your statement. Then you may go, Miss Torgerson," the sergeant declared, clearing his throat. "Officer Odegaard will take it from you." He gave a nod to the officer.

"I think it's important that I debrief Miss Torgerson, don't you?" George asked softly.

"That'll work." Sinclair glanced at officer Odegaard. "Round up a few more men. Let's go" Sergeant Sinclair rose from behind his desk and left, with Odegaard following.

"I was on the train as a backup for Captain Healy," George said to Brita. She nodded. It was all so unreal. George leaned forward. "Let's start from the top, shall we?"

"First, will you send a message to the train so they hold my job and don't leave without me?" Brita asked. Her head started to pound, and it took all of her strength to not break down and cry.

"Sure." George reached for the telephone and began to dial the depot.

Brita's thoughts went to Denver—she'd get a room and sleep until the next year without any disturbance. When he hung up the phone, she braced herself for reliving the entire story.

"Let's begin. You'll feel better once it's off your chest." George picked up a pad and pencil. "Whenever you're ready."

"It started with the murder in Chicago." Her eyes met his, and she warmed to his friendly demeanor. "This has been a terrible ordeal."

"Take your time." Listening, George sat back and wrote as the story unfolded from the Twin Cities Zephyr to Chicago, getting on the Burlington Zephyr, and bringing him up to the present moment. He had interjected questions as needed. "How was it that the gun went off tonight and killed Swensen?"

"I went straight up to Swensen with my gun, which my father had given me, and he flicked his cigarette into my face. I shot the gun off accidentally and nicked his foot, and my gun skidded into the street. Then the guard, Scott, held up his gun as Swensen pulled me in front of him. I struggled as we both reached for the gun. Scott, it turns out, didn't have any bullets. Anyway, we both reached for my gun, and in the struggle I shot him in the neck. He went down. That's all." She blew her nose.

"What did he say? Anything at all?" George leaned closer.

"He spoke in German. It was, let's see… first he said, 'Du Nutte', then his last words were, 'Der Mohr hat seine Schuldigkeit getan' and then it was, 'alles is vorbei.' It was a faint whisper, but that's what I understood."

"What does that mean?" George drummed his knee in anticipation.

"'Bitch. The deed's done. The Moor has done what he had to do… the Moor go to hell.'" Brita nodded to reconfirm to herself that she'd translated it correctly. "I'm not sure what that means, but that's what he said… at least what I was able to understand."

"Our worst fears. He did poison the grain." He gasped. "It means that now it's over."

"Oh my God. Ron—I mean Captain Healy—was correct in his suspicions," she said, raising a brow. She shook her head and gulped. "Maybe killing him wasn't so bad after all."

"Killing is never right, but sometimes it's necessary. War brings out the worst in people. Anything more to add?" He raised a brow and waited.

"I started pawing through his satchel when I saw Ron… I mean Captain Healy, come over. That's all." She took a deep breath and looked into his eyes. "Now may I go?"

"Yes, that wraps it up. You did great. Thanks for being so cooperative. How about I get a policeman to drive you to the train?" He gave her a smile as he rose.

"Thanks." Brita stood and glanced out the window. "I can't believe this has happened. I'm glad it's over."

"Me, too." He got up and reached for the door, motioning for a policeman to come over. After he'd ordered him to take Brita to the station, George turned to Brita. "Shall we?"

He held the door open and they stepped out into the hallway.

"Don't worry anymore, Brita, you'll be fine," George said, shaking her hand. "I'll inform your father that you're going to Denver. Thank you for your help."

"Thank you."

Brita walked out the front door and down the steps to where a squad car sat with the engine running and a policeman waiting.

George leaned into the window. "Officer, please pick up Captain Healy's belongings and bring them back here. Leave them in the sergeant's office. Understand?"

"Yes, sir."

On the way to the Zephyr, Brita's thoughts churned round and round about the questioning. She wondered why George needed to know exactly where Swensen sat, whom he talked to, and his hand gestures or facial expressions. He had wanted to know if Swensen pulled on his ear at all, or winked at anyone. It all seemed crazy. Brita thought over Mindel and Swensen, and hoped that she'd explained or answered questions well enough for George. She certainly didn't want to be questioned again.

Brita glanced at the officer as he drove the car right up beside the depot and parked.

"Here we are, miss," he said. Glancing at her, he gave a quick smile. "Have a good trip." The policeman came around and opened the door. "Where might I find the conductor?"

"Thank you," she said before climbing out of the car. "Follow me."

Brita looked up at the depot, and thought of how small it was compared to the Chicago station. But when she entered the main doors, she realized that one station was really no different from another.

The public intercom system blared.

All aboard! Passengers riding the Zephyr to Denver are asked to board on track number nine! The Zephyr leaves in thirty minutes! Alllllllll aboooooooooooard!

Brita glanced at the wall clock and it read six-thirty.

All aboard! Passengers on the Topeka and Omaha traveling for San Francisco! Alllllllll aboard! Platform number five! Allllllll aboooooooooooard!

She walked quickly out the doors and headed toward the loading platform with the policeman following her.

Stan was busy checking in bags, and they walked over to him.

"I bet you want Healy's bag? It's right here," Stan said. He reached over and handed it to the officer.

"Thanks." The officer took it and walked away.

"Brita, I've wondered about you." His bright smile warmed her heart as he looked at her.

"I'm back." Brita gave him a big smile. "I'm going to work this next shift." She had a hard time suppressing a yawn.

"'Bout time my Zephyrette returned. Good. Now go and get ready for the trip. Sometime in between, we'll have a little talk."

"Thanks," Brita said above the noise.

"I'll find you later." Stan turned to an approaching passenger. "Tickets, ma'am?"

As Brita stepped inside of the Zephyr, she let out a long yawn. Gladys wasn't in sight, and Brita didn't want to see her until she was cleaned up. She headed right for her compartment.

While walking down the corridor, she glanced outside. Omaha really was a bustling town. The sun was beginning to rise high in the sky, casting shadows across the roofs of the tall buildings that surrounded the stockyards. Brita breathed deeply to clear her head from the smells and sounds from the stockyard. Soon, she was at her cabin.

After closing her door, Brita let out a long sigh and leaned into the door. Brita's heart beat wildly when her thoughts went to pulling the trigger and killing Swensen. Tears filled her eyes, and she welcomed them as she clutched her chest. She sank onto the bed and cried as all of her pent-up emotions—including her feelings about Ron—were released.

"I thought his kiss meant something. I thought we might have had a future," she said, sighing. Brita tried to block out the realization that Ron had tricked her. He had been an agent and had used that as an excuse to get close to her... when in actuality, he was just doing his job. She gripped the handkerchief tight and succumbed to grief as new tears for a love lost filled her eyes. Her heart felt like a fragile teacup that had just shattered into a million pieces.

A knock on the door made her jump.

"Yes?" Brita stammered, and hoped it wasn't Stan.

"Brita?" Dwight stood poised and ready to lightly knock again. "Are you okay in there?" He listened as she moved around inside of the room.

"Just a minute." Brita quickly looked into the mirror and groaned, but was relieved that it was Dwight.

She blew her nose. "Dwight? I need to clean up and then I'll be ready. Is that okay?" Brita chose to talk through the door because she didn't want anyone to see her. "Will you bring me a cup of strong coffee?"

"Sure, I'll be right back."

Brita took the few minutes to comb through her tangled hair. She took out a fresh set of underwear and silk stockings and lay them on the bed. As she reached for her clean uniform, there was a knock on the door.

"Yes?"

"It's the coffee boy," Dwight said, grinning.

"Thanks." She gave him a big smile. "I'll start working as soon as I clean up."

"The train will start for Denver in less than ten minutes. Will that give you enough time?"

"Yes. Thank you." Brita shut the door.

The hot soapy water felt good as she scrubbed and washed her hair, then gave herself a sponge bath. She sprayed herself liberally with perfume to help block out the imaginary stockyard smell. The fresh clean uniform perked up her spirits. When she thought about the approaching evening, the first thing that crossed her mind was sitting and soaking in a hot tub of water.

Before stepping out, she applied fresh lipstick and ran a comb through her hair. She took one last look in the mirror, and still saw roadmaps for eyes.

As she stepped out the door, the train began jolting and jerking as it left the depot.

This is the conductor of the Great Burlington Zephyr. We will be in Denver's Union Station in seven hours! Enjoy your ride and the beautiful scenery!

The train started to pick up speed as it rolled through the intersections. Brita took a moment to look over at the stockyards. As the train passed them by, she stared over at the crime scene and saw several policemen and squad cars. She didn't see Ron, but told herself that he was out of her life anyway. She glanced up at the tower and saw Scott. She waved, but was sure that he hadn't seen her.

As soon as the stockyards were out of view, Brita drew in a deep breath. When she exhaled, she forced herself to look away.

With each footstep, she told herself that Ron was no different than her other boyfriends. The train seemed to rock and roll, and the rhythm lifted her spirits and gave her more determination. It didn't take long until she was through the sleeping cars and entering the vestibule into the lounge car.

Brita felt like a new person.

As she approached the lounge car, her resolve to banish Ron from her mind had taken hold. When her hand gripped the handle, she felt her stomach quiver. The room unfolded in front of her, and she saw Gladys.

Gladys was a welcome sight, and also a lifesaver. Brita didn't have to look at the bar if she was looking at her friend.

She held her head high and went right over to Gladys.

"Toots! Where on earth have you been? Did you know that there was a killer on board? And that he was going to blow up the train?" Gladys bobbed her head and winked as she placed an arm over Brita's shoulder. "There's been so much excitement."

"Tell me all about it. I'm dying to hear." It was great to be back on the job. With Gladys around, Brita would hear all the gossip.

Brita kept one ear open to listen, but she let her mind wander. She looked out on the prairie, watching it as it rolled past.

The farmland was dotted with threshing machines and tall water windmills. Wheat fields blew in the wind as far as the eye could see. Two-story farmhouses sat beside the barns, chicken coops, and pasture like a country postcard. In the distance, Brita saw a flag waving.

She smiled and looked back at Gladys.

"I'd best be on my rounds," Brita said. "Which car should I go to first?"

"The observation deck."

Brita left and hoped that she'd soon see Ella.

Chapter Twenty

Ron heaved back into a chair in the sergeant's office. George was seated across from him, and he shut his eyes and sighed.

"Never thought this would happen," Ron said wearily. "I'm pooped with a capital 'P'."

"Me, too," George said, reluctantly opening his eyes. "I'm sure glad that I called Doctor Bendsen right off the bat and got him here. We'd still be wondering about the toxin in the feed." He shook his head and glanced out the window. "The sun's setting."

"I need a hot bath, a good stiff drink, a huge steak dinner, and a bed. But not necessarily in that order." Ron suppressed a yawn. "I hope it's not just me that stinks."

"I think a Scotch is in order. I wonder if the good sergeant has anything hidden?" George glanced around the room in hopes of seeing a bottle out in the open.

"How long do you reckon it'll take them to surge the contaminated grain to a different site, and then for the cleaning crew to remove all the residue?" Ron asked, raising a brow. "Probably a week," he said, answering his own question. "Has the Chicago bureau checked in at all?"

"Oh yeah!" George reached into his pocket and took out the message. "The elevator has been shut down, and they're checking the grain there now." He gave Ron a curious smile. "Isn't there a song that says, 'it can only happen to me'?"

"What about Burlington, and old Ole? Any confirmation there?" Ron asked. "Oops! Never mind, that's in my pocket. I almost forgot." He pulled out the message and yawned fiercely. "Jeez, I'm tired." With a flick of his wrist, the paper opened. "Ole has traced Swensen's movements and identified a handful of people who are now under surveillance, and an arrest is imminent."

"Good," George said. "Everything is getting wrapped up tight. We could've had a real blown-out mess on our hands."

"I'll say. The entire beef supply could've been poisoned. That would have changed the entire course of the war. Bloody awful," Ron said.

"Yeah, the troops would've had to eat canned horsemeat or Spam." George grinned.

"With an extra package of sugar to sweeten the smell and horseradish for flavor." He looked over to the corner and saw that his bag was sitting there. "I see that all of my belongings were sent for."

"Yes. Dwight wanted to know if the large brown dress was really yours." George grinned. "I'm sure you looked like proper sailor bait." He yawned and stretched before leaning back in the chair. "I see that my bag is still parked over there in the corner. Right where I dropped it many, many hours ago." George sat up straighter as a thought occurred to him. "By the way, has it been confirmed that Swensen killed the man in Chicago?"

"Yes, I believe so. For the murder here, he used the tie as a garrote and placed a coin in the mouth, which linked him to Rose. The same tie was used on Rose, and a similar one was left near Mindel. In all accounts, except Fortier, a tie was present. Swensen's presence has been documented, except in Minneapolis. That's the information that the bureau has told me. With Fortier's death, I believed Brita would have been next." Ron heaved a sigh of relief.

"Has the Zephyr left?"

"What are you talking about?" Suddenly Ron's eyes opened wide, and he whispered, "Brita…"

"Yep. I think she's given you the boot." George stood up and stared out the window. "I don't hear a train whistle."

"It's gone. Brita's gone? My assignment is to be on that train as an undercover agent." Ron gulped and gave George a blank stare. "Now what?"

"It's your job. If I were you, I'd start hustling."

Ron raced to the door, giving George a quick salute. "Have a safe trip."

*****

Brita climbed the stairs to the observation deck and saw farmland for as far as the eye could see. All the different shades of fall colors met her eye. Autumn gold and yellow from the wheat, rye, and oat fields blanketed the earth. Stubbled cornfields added texture to the harvest colors.

Between the rows and rows of crops, farm machinery clipped and threshed grain. Large fields of hay lay ready for picking and storage for large animal winter feeding.

The seats were filled with businessmen, women wearing heavy wool dresses, and soldiers, mostly in Air Force uniforms.

"Care for a magazine, sir?" she asked the nearest gentleman. "I can get you one straightaway." Brita gave him a quick smile.

"No, thank you, miss. I'm enjoying the scenery." He rested his eyes on her for a second before looking back out the windows.

After Brita had walked through the entire car answering questions and fetching magazines or newspapers, she headed down the stairs.

It jolted her when she entered the lounge. There was a stranger manning the bar. It took her by surprise, even though she knew that Ron wouldn't be there.

Women stood around the poker tables as the men played. Smoke circled above their heads while voices — loud and soft — offered their bets. Brita walked over to the tables.

"Does anyone need any help? Can I get a drink for anyone?" she asked. Brita's legs were beginning to buzz from all the walking, and the night before was taking its toll. She was tired.

"Yes ma'am. I'll have another gin and tonic. Here's the cash," a man said. He handed her his glass.

"Anyone else?" she asked, giving them each a smile. When they shook their heads, Brita took the money and glass before going after the drink.

Brita hurried over to the bar, and, forgetting how the train would occasionally do a double two-step, almost fell. She reprimanded herself for not being more careful. After getting the refill, she brought it over to the gentleman.

As Brita headed for the dining car, the overhead speaker crackled and snapped. She stopped a moment to listen.

This is the conductor. In another four hours, we will be entering the beautiful city of Denver, Colorado. Before we leave the wonderful state of Nebraska, I'd like to point out will announce a few points of interest.

The Pulitzer Prize winning author, Willa Cather, came from Red Cloud. She wrote several books, but the Pulitzer went to her novel, One of Ours. It was written in 1922.

Chimney Rock, a junction of the Oregon and Mormon Trails. Have a great day, and enjoy your ride on the great Zephyr!

Brita continued through the corridor. As she entered the dining car, Harold stood facing her. A smile crossed his face when she looked at him.

"I've been waiting all day to see you," he said. "My wife is doing fine. I have a baby girl, and will soon be home and having a week's vacation. I get to be a dad!" He grinned from ear to ear.

"Good for you." She smiled back. "Congratulations to you and your wife. What did you name her? Wiggles and Cutie-pie come to mind." She chuckled.

"I was thinking more along the lines of Honeydew." He laughed. "I must get busy. Want to get the folks some water and help me pass out the food? I'm shorthanded."

"Will do." Brita went straight to the sink and filled a pitcher. As she filled the passengers' water glasses, her thoughts went to the night before. She wondered about Ron, catching herself thinking wistfully about his kiss until someone interrupted her thoughts with a request. "Yes sir, I'll bring fresh coffee."

When she was finished in the dining car, Brita hiked back through the cars toward the large passenger car where the mothers sat.

Brita performed her duties methodically. Suddenly, the overhead speaker came alive again. Brita plunked into an empty chair to listen, noticing that the horizon outside the window had become rich with snowy mountain peaks.

This is the conductor. We will be arriving on time at the Union Depot in the lovely town of Denver in two hours. Please finish your dinner and prepare for the stop.

However, if you plan to stay, take the time to visit the gravesite of Buffalo Bill on Lookout Mountain, right outside of Denver. Or maybe try your luck in panning for gold. Enjoy the rest of the ride. Over and out.

Brita got up and headed for the observation deck after taking care of a few passengers. When she was ready to climb the stairs, she noticed Stan heading her way.

"Do you have time for a talk?" he asked. "We need to discuss your employment." He motioned to the nearest empty compartment.

Brita entered and Stan followed, closing the door behind him.

"What are your thoughts? So many things have happened to you, Brita, that I wonder if you even want to work?" He stood with his hand on the knob and looked down at her.

"I think I need a break. Too much has been going on for me to know whether I even like being a Zephyrette. I'm going to take some time to think. Is that okay?" She looked up at him, hoping that he wouldn't tell her that she couldn't come back.

"I think that's for the best. I'll tell the Burlington people that you're taking time off and that you'll contact them when you're ready to resume working." He gave her a slight nod. "I wish you well."

"Thank you." Brita stood.

Stan held the door, and they walked out.

The compartment cars were packed with women and children. Right away, she had orders for tea and coffee and pie. Once she got everything served, she changed diapers for a mother of twin boys.

Afterward, Brita went to the passenger car and spent time answering questions about the ride and the time schedule. Two gentlemen requested the paper, and she went after them, and brought an ashtray for one of them.

Brita walked up to the observation deck and saw her friend Ella busy knitting.

"Hi! It's been awhile," Brita said, sitting beside her. "Can I get you anything?"

"Nope. I'm going to start working real soon at the radio station, and need to get this sweater done. Say! What about you?"

"Do you happen to know of a real good hotel that has room service and a hot bath in the room?" Brita yawned.

"Yep. Go the Ambassador Hotel. It's new, and they'll treat you right." She kept the needles clicking. "I might go there myself, but I'm not sure. I want to be close to the station."

"Thanks. Good luck! I hope to hear you on the radio." Brita chuckled and walked away.

As the train began slowing down, a plan formulated in her mind. First a taxi, then the bath, and then room service… and maybe another bath.

The overhead public-address speaker crackled on.

We will be arriving in ten minutes. Get ready to view the lovely town of Denver. Thank you for traveling the Zephyr. Over and out.

When everyone was off the train, Brita said goodbye to Gladys, who was returning to Chicago in the morning. Dwight handed her her suitcase and told her that he'd also be returning to Chicago.

Brita stepped into awaiting cab and requested that the driver to take her to the Ambassador Hotel.

*****

Ron climbed onboard the Chicago-Burlington and Quincy line that headed straight for Denver. He felt lucky. At least he hadn't had to make any changes between the Omaha and Denver, which gave him time to think about Brita. Glancing at his watch, he grinned. Pending any problems, he'd be in Denver at about five in the morning. It was 8:00 p.m. now. Since he couldn't get on the next Zephyr, he knew that his train would be slower and would make more stops.

His thoughts drifted to how she'd managed to slip out from under his nose.

Before he had left the depot, he'd wired the general and told him in brief terms what had happened, and that Brita had felt compelled to finish her run on the Zephyr. He also told the general that he was on his way to Denver to carry out the rest of his assignment.

As the train moved out of the station, Ron wished that this train had a lounge. He hadn't bought a sleeping berth because he knew he wouldn't be able to sleep anyway. Brita had that effect on him.

He went directly to the nearest compartment and sat on the bench. Fortunately, he was alone. There was a two-day-old Denver newspaper beside him, and he reached for it.

As he thumbed through the pages, he wondered where Brita would stay the night. Ron circled three hotels to contact and wrote the name and addresses down in his notebook. He shoved the paper aside and took a sip of his drink, letting his mind wander to Brita and the night before in her room.

It was hard to believe that it had been a mere twenty-four hours since he'd held her in his arms. She'd smelled so good, and when he thought of her kisses, he felt a sensation that he'd never felt before. Her skin was so soft and tender, and her eyes were as blue as the sky. Her voice was almost magical, and he couldn't fathom never hearing it again. He leaned back in the seat, shut his eyes, and pictured her standing in front of him.

The slowing of the wheels and the train's whistle woke him. Ron yawned and stretched and looked out at the mountains as the train rolled to a stop in the Burlington depot.

With his bag in hand, Ron was the first in line to step off the train.

The brisk fresh morning air was refreshing. He hailed the first cab.

"Hotel Roosevelt," Ron said, climbing inside of the vehicle.

"Yes, sir." The cab driver glanced at Ron before pulling away from the curb. "You look tired."

"I am. Now hurry."

As Ron was whisked down the street, he tried to think of what to say to Brita, but came up empty. He pondered over the puzzle as the driver pulled up next to the curb.

"Wait right here," he said to the cabbie. "I'm just popping inside for a minute. Got it?

"Yes sir." The cab driver waited as Ron stepped through the main doors. It didn't take long to find out that Brita wasn't there.

"Shoot," Ron grumbled to himself on the way out. He climbed into the cab again. "The Cosmopolitan, straightaway. And hurry." Ron looked at his watch and grimaced. It was already 6:30. Brita could be getting ready to leave.

"Yes, sir," the cab driver replied. He put the car in drive and stepped on the gas.

Ron stared out the window and searched the face of every woman he saw, looking for Brita. Unfortunately, they all reminded him of her, and he thought he was going to go nuts.

"Here we are, sir. Should I wait?"

"Yes, of course."

Ron slammed the car door and thought about how stupid the driver was as he entered the Cosmopolitan lobby.

After getting a shake of the head, showing his badge and having a quick look at the roster of guests, Ron grunted a "thank you" and left.

"Ambassador, and make it quick," Ron growled at the cab driver as he slammed the door. "No stopping for anything. That's an order."

"Yes, sir. What are you, some kind of copper?"

"Yes. Now go." Ron sat back and mentally tried to rehearse what he was going to say, but no words came to mind. Consciously, he felt his arm holster and gun and in his side pocket he felt Brita's derringer. He knew she had every right to mad. She did have to finish the trip, after all.

"Here we are sir," the cab driver said. He parked in front of the door.

"Wait right here," Ron said, jumping out of the cab.

"I figured that out already."

As Ron entered the lobby, he reached into his pocket for his badge. He showed it to the attendant and asked to see the list of guests. The sight of Brita's name made his heart pound hard.

He went back out to the cab, paid the driver, and grabbed his bag.

Entering the lobby again, he headed for the main desk and asked for the phone line to the kitchen.

"I'd like to place an order for two for room number two-fifteen… yes, two orders of eggs, bacon, toast, and coffee. Thank you. How long?"

"Fifteen minutes."

"Thank you. Oh, and one apple strudel. Thanks." Ron hung up the phone and headed for the kitchen.

Inside the main door was a small closet. Checking to see whether anyone was watching, he took out a bellboy jacket and vest and quickly slipped them over his arm, then headed toward the elevator.

Beside the elevator was a huge spray of flowers. From it, he took a long-stemmed rose, and waited until a busboy appeared with his breakfast order.

"That's the two orders of bacon and eggs? Here." Ron paid for the food and handed the busboy a large tip. "I'll take it from here. I know the room." He pushed the trolley cart onto the elevator and headed for room 215.

Arriving at the door, Ron slipped his satchel and jacket onto the shelf under the trolley. Placing Brita's derringer and the stolen rose on the tray, he slipped into the vest and jacket before taking a deep breath.

He tapped lightly on the door. "Room service!" He tapped again. His heart beat hard, and it felt like it would jump out of his chest until at last he heard her sweet voice.

"I didn't order room service."

"It's on the house."

"Just a minute."

Chapter Twenty-One

Day Seven

The voice had a familiar ring to it, but Brita's head was still foggy from sleep. She opened the door and peeked out.

Ron stood outside the open door.

"Brita." He gave her a smile. When he saw her golden locks falling over her brow, he thought of a halo.

"Who are you? Or should I say, what are you today?" Brita asked before slamming the door and wondering why the sight of him still made her heart pound. Leaning into the door, she inhaled deeply and let out a long, exasperated breath. As she did, he pounded again.

"Brita? Let's eat. We can talk over the meal," Ron called through the door. He rapped again. "Please."

Brita's cheeks grew pink with embarrassment. Knowing she'd never get rid of him, she called through the door, "Just a minute." However, she wasn't quite sure how to address him, since this was the *third* persona he'd adopted since they'd met.

After smoothing her hair down, she realized what she was wearing and who was waiting, and felt the blush moving down her throat. She dressed quickly.

Ron let out his own exasperated sigh as he waited, counting the minutes until she opened the door.

"Well… come in." She opened the door, and watched his face fall as he saw how she was dressed. Her hair was covered with a scarf tied under her chin. The dress she wore fell to the floor and covered her feet, and the long sleeves dangled. "What do you want, Mister… bartender, OSS agent? Or is your new job a busboy? Which is it? I need to know, Mr. Healy." She stood with her hands on her hips as he rolled the cart into the room. "I see that you brought my gun. How kind of you."

Ignoring the sarcasm, Ron lifted the covers from the plates. "Let's eat. It smells good." He waved the covers to breathe in the full aroma, then set the food on the table.

"You're incorrigible." Brita plunked into the chair opposite his and lifted a fork.

"To us." Ron raised his cup of coffee. "Aren't you going to toast us, since we worked so well together?" He grinned. When she didn't raise her cup for a toast but simply drank, he did also. He cleared his throat before beginning to eat. "You look lovely in your new dress and hairdo."

"You're an idiot. So, Mr. Healy, you never did tell me… who are you today?" Brita began to eat, avoiding looking at him. She hated to admit it, but he was still the most handsome man in the world. As she watched him eat out of the corner of her eye, Brita also knew that she wanted his lips pressed against hers forever. Then her mind jolted her back to the present, and she remembered that he was conniving, deceitful, and a liar.

She decided to march him right out of the room as fast as possible.

"Brita? You… ah… seem to have something smudged on your right cheek." Ron watched as she rubbed at the imaginary smudge.

"Better?" Brita gave him a stern look. When he shook his head, she used her linen to napkin to wipe it off.

"Here. Let me help you." Ron took his napkin and reached across the table. Brita grabbed his arm.

"Don't you touch me." When their eyes met, they continued to stare at each other for a moment before Brita looked away.

"Is the strudel good?" Ron whispered, wiping her cheek. He pulled off her scarf and tossed it on the bed. Her curls sprung out and waved around her face, which took his breath away. "Much better."

"Yes, the strudel is very good." She didn't want to let him

know that she was starting to soften, or that she enjoyed looking at him. "So tell me Mr. Healy, why are you so deceitful?" Brita took the gun off the tray and placed it beside her on the table.

"Let's finish eating before we begin our discussion, shall we?" Ron slowly ate as he watched her fidget. He sure wanted to kiss her.

They finished eating in silence. Then, in unison, they shoved their plates aside, and both reached for their coffee cups.

"I don't have time for idle chit-chat, Mr. Healy, so drink up and get out." Brita had a terrible time calming her beating heart.

"What are your plans, Brita?" Ron set his cup down and stared at her.

"It's Miss Torgerson to you, Mr. Healy." She looked him straight in the eye. "You're explaining why you kept your true identity a secret. Then I'll let you know what my plans are."

"Fair enough," Ron said. After telling his story, which included the infamous line from her father, he concluded by saying, "Now, are you satisfied?"

"Yes."

"A bottle of champagne is in order," Ron said.

"I hope you'll enjoy your ten fingers before they're all broken."

www.ingramcontent.com/pod-product-compliance
Lightning Source LLC
Chambersburg PA
CBHW070503120726
47910CB00003B/1105